Barbara Cartland, the w... novelist, who is also an histo... cal speaker and television p... 390 books and sold over 370 ...

She has also had many historical works published and has written four autobiographies as well as the biographies of her mother and that of her brother, Ronald Cartland, who was the first Member of Parliament to be killed in the last war. This book has a preface by Sir Winston Churchill and has just been republished with an introduction by Sir Arthur Bryant.

Love at the Helm, a novel written with the help and inspiration of the late Earl Mountbatten of Burma, Uncle of His Royal Highness Prince Philip, is being sold for the Mountbatten Memorial Trust.

Miss Cartland in 1978 sang an Album of Love Songs with the Royal Philharmonic Orchestra.

In 1976 by writing twenty-one books, she broke the world record and has continued for the following seven years with 24, 20, 23, 24, 24 25 and 23. In The *Guinness Book of Records* she is listed as the world's top-selling author.

In private life Barbara Cartland, who is a Dame of Grace of the Order of St. John of Jerusalem, Chairman of the St. John Council in Hertfordshire and Deputy President of the St. John Ambulance Brigade, has fought for better conditions and salaries for Midwives and Nurses.

She has championed the cause for old people, had the law altered regarding gypsies and founded the first Romany Gypsy camp in the world.

Barbara Cartland is deeply interested in Vitamin therapy and is President of the National Association for Health.

Her designs "Decorating with Love" are being sold all over the U.S.A. and the National Home Fashions League made her, in 1981, "Woman of Achievement".

Barbara Cartland's Romances (Book of Cartoons) has been published in Great Britain, and the U.S.A as has her *Romance of Food* and *Getting Older, Growing Younger*.

For other titles by Barbara Cartland please see pages 159, 160.

BARBARA CARTLAND

TEMPTATION FOR A TEACHER

Pan Original
Pan Books London and Sydney

First published 1985 by Pan Books Ltd,
Cavaye Place, London SW10 9PG
9 8 7 6 5 4 3 2 1
© Cartland Promotions 1985
ISBN 0 330 28750 8
Photoset by Parker Typesetting Service, Leicester
Printed and bound in Great Britain by
Collins, Glasgow

Author's note

When I visited France in 1983, I motored to the mountainous, fertile Dordogne. Passing along a narrow roadway I saw a magnificent medieval Castle, rising above a small river, very ancient but obviously still inhabited.

We drove closer and found behind it a very small attractive village with a lovely Twelfth Century Church exactly as I describe in this novel.

That night we stayed in a very old Castle which had been converted into a hotel. My circular bedroom was in the Tower. It had a beamed ceiling and small windows in a three-foot thick wall, from which there was a panoramic view of the countryside.

Beneath me I was sure there were dark, dark dungeons! This story was born before I fell asleep.

Arletta was the name of William the Conqueror's mother who came from Normandy, and his grandfather, Duke Rollo had three sons who were Kings of England.

The Granvilles, who are one of the oldest and most famous families in England, can trace their ancestry directly back to Duke Rollo. Through their father's mother, my two sons are related to him, and so incidently through her Great-Grandfather is the Princess of Wales.

Chapter One
1886

"I'm sorry, Lady Arletta. I'm afraid it gives you very little time."

"Very little, Mr Metcalfe."

Lady Arletta Cherrington-Weir gave a deep sigh and her blue eyes were wistful.

Mr Metcalfe, a precise, middle-aged Solicitor, thought that if it were in his power he would do anything to sweep away the worried look on her face.

He had known Lady Arletta since she was an infant in a perambulator and had watched her grow up, becoming in doing so, more lovely year by year.

He thought now it was impossible for any young woman of twenty to be more beautiful and at the same time completely unselfconscious and unaware of her own attractions.

This, however, was not surprising considering that for the past two years Lady Arletta had been obliged to nurse her father the Earl of Weir, who had grown month by month increasingly querulous and disagreeable.

He had refused to have anybody else to attend on him and treated his daughter, as the Doctors and everybody else thought, as he would not have dared to treat a professional Nurse.

But Nurses were exceedingly difficult to find, and in the quiet Counties of England, and especially in the villages, there were no nursing facilities except for the village Midwife who was usually old and fat, and reputed to keep herself awake by imbibing through the dark hours of the night large tots of gin.

Arletta therefore had been obliged to nurse her father

who was suffering not only from heart attacks, which gave him excruciating pain, but also from gout, which was entirely due to the amount of Claret and Port he insisted on drinking despite the protests of his Physicians.

"If I have to die," he would say angrily, "I may as well have the comfort of feeling drunk, and I am damned if I will have the only solace for my disgusting condition taken away from me."

Arletta had long ago given up arguing with him. She merely agreed with everything he said, and then he swore at her for being dull and spiritless.

Actually in his better moods he was exceedingly fond of his only child, although it was a bitter disappointment there was no son to inherit the Earldom.

It would therefore pass on to his nephew, whom inevitably he disliked.

Arletta did not like Hugo either, thinking him a conceited young man who had his own ideas as to how he would run the estate and who refused to listen to anything his Uncle or she could tell him about it.

Now, two weeks after her father's death, Arletta had been told that her cousin intended to move at once into Weir House and she was to remove herself and her belongings as quickly as possible.

The trouble was, as she had said to Mr Metcalfe, she did not know where to go.

"You must have some relative with whom you could stay, My Lady," he expostulated, "and of course, if you wish, you can always live in the Dower House."

"I know that," Arletta replied, "and it is very kind of Cousin Hugo to offer it to me. But you know as well as I do, Mr Metcalfe, that I would not be allowed to live there alone."

She sighed before she went on;

"And I do not think I could bear to see my cousin turn the whole estate upside-down and manage it in quite a different way from Papa's methods."

"I am sure you would be wise to go elsewhere," Mr Metcalfe said quietly, "but because of your father's illness, you were not presented at Court, as you should have been, a year ago, and you never had the Ball which I know you were looking forward to long before you left the School-Room."

Arletta smiled.

"I always imagined my Ball at Weir House would be a particularly splendid one. Mama used to talk about it when I was quite small, and say that it would be the best the County had ever seen, and like the times when my grandfather was alive."

Mr Metcalfe was well aware that it was the Third Earl who had dissipated with unbridled extravagance the Weir fortune, and plunged the estate heavily into debt.

The late Earl had done his best to develop the land, make the farms pay, and to ensure that they lived within their means.

But he could not bring back into the family Exchequer the revenue from the streets and squares of London which had been sold for what now seemed a pittance, and the money which had been squandered by speculating in 'get-rich-quick' schemes which never materialised.

When he had fallen seriously ill just at the time when Arletta was emerging from the School-Room, all ideas of entertainment had been set to one side.

As he was extremely disagreeable to those who called to commiserate with him, he and his daughter became more and more isolated in the great house which seemed unnaturally quiet after years of being filled with guests and a great deal of activity.

Since the Earl could no longer ride, the foxhounds had been taken over by another landowner in the County; the Fête which was one of the great local pleasures of the summer was held elsewhere; and the Archery Competition no longer took place on the long green lawns.

The whole estate then seemed to be enveloped in a fog

9

of depression and anticipation as to how long the Earl would live.

It was, in fact, due to his daughter's care that he had lived longer than expected, but now the end had come and Mr Metcalfe thought optimistically that it might be a beginning for Lady Arletta.

"Now let us think this over sensibly," he said in a business-like voice. "I know all your relatives, and I hope you will not think it impertinent of me if I suggest who I think would look after you best and make you happy."

"Of course, dear Mr Metcalfe. I will be grateful for any suggestion you can make," Arletta replied. "The trouble is, as you well know, I have very few close relatives living in England."

The Earl's youngest brother, who was actually very much younger than the Earl, was Governor of Khartoum, and as he was unmarried it was not likely that he would want his niece to stay with him in such an isolated and troubled place for any length of time.

Her only Aunt on the other hand was married to the Governor of the North-West Provinces in India.

As she already had three daughters of her own and found them a problem, Mr Metcalfe was quite certain she would have no wish to have Lady Arletta added to her responsibilities.

There was a long pause before he said:

"My Lady, there is your Cousin Emily."

Arletta gave a little cry of horror.

"I will not live with Cousin Emily, Mr Metcalfe! That would be too unkind. You know how she is given to good works, and she disapproves of everything such as dancing and singing, even if people are happy. I cannot think of anything more depressing than having to live with Cousin Emily!"

Mr Metcalfe laughed.

"I agree with you, Lady Arletta, so we must think of somebody else."

"But who?"

Arletta gave a little sigh before she added;

"I have often wished that I knew some of my grand-mother's relatives, but because they were French they never seemed to come to England, and although I was called after her, I have never been to France."

"That is something I had forgotten," Mr Metcalfe murmured. "Of course, Arletta is a French name."

"I have always been told that it was the name of William the Conqueror's mother," Arletta said, "and because Grandmama came from Normandy, she had fair hair and blue eyes. So although I look English, I also look French."

Mr Metcalfe laughed.

"I am prepared to believe you, Lady Arletta, although I always think of Frenchwomen as having dark eyes and dark hair."

"Not if they are Normans!" Arletta said proudly.

Then she went on:

"Unless I am to write to Grandmama's relatives whom I have never seen, who is there in England?"

"There is Lady Travers," Mr Metcalfe suggested.

Arletta made a little grimace.

Lady Travers was a cousin who in the past had occasionally visited Weir House, but only when she invited herself.

She was the type of middle-aged woman who was always suffering from some strange and unknown complaint which puzzled the Doctors. Arletta had decided a long time ago that the only thing that was wrong with her Cousin Alice was that she had not enough to do.

She had enough money to live in great comfort, but she had no children, and she therefore concentrated entirely on herself and her ailments.

She would spend months in Harrogate, then Cheltenham, until finding she was no better in either of these places, she would move on to Bath, or just occasionally some Spa like Baden-Baden, or Aix-les-Bains.

Arletta thought that after two years of coping with one invalid in the shape of her father it would be utter misery to start all over again with another.

Mr Metcalfe watching her face knew what she was thinking.

"Definitely not Lady Travers!" he said firmly. "I am trying to remember who else there is."

"That is what I was doing before you arrived," Arletta said, "but I find it hard to believe that in such a distinguished family as ours there are so few of us left."

"There must be somebody," Mr Metcalfe said desperately.

"I have some relatives who live in the very North of Scotland," Arletta answered, "and I believe there is a distant branch of the family in Ireland, but I cannot imagine they would be very pleased to see me after Papa has ignored them for so long."

As this was palpably true, Mr Metcalfe did not even trouble to agree.

He merely sat doodling on the block in front of him and seeing in his mind's eye the impressive Family Tree which hung in the passage near to the Library.

Arletta suddenly jumped up from her chair.

"It is no use worrying at the moment," she said. "I will move my things into the Dower House until I can think of somewhere where I can go."

"You ought to be in London, My Lady," Mr Metcalfe said. "After all, the Season has only just begun, and there must be somebody, even though you are in mourning, who would see that you met young people of your own age."

"You say I am in mourning," Arletta replied, "but you will remember that in Papa's Will he said expressly that nobody was to wear black, nobody was to mourn for him, and the sooner he was dead, the better he would be pleased!"

Mr Metcalfe, who had drawn up the Will himself and

thought it was just the sort of thing the Earl would say, did not reply.

At the time it had seemed rather bad taste, and he felt now that spoken in Arletta's soft, musical voice it sounded almost cruel.

"No one could have worked harder than you, My Lady," he said quietly, "to make your father happy in the last year of his life, and I am well aware what a difficult patient he was."

"Terrible!" Arletta agreed.

Quite unexpectedly she laughed before she went on:

"The Doctors could do nothing with him and neither could I. I think the only pleasure he had when he was in such pain was to defy us and do exactly the opposite of what was required of him."

"I am afraid the late Earl was always a rebel," Mr Metcalfe sighed.

"I hope I am one too," Arletta remarked.

Mr Metcalfe looked at her in surprise, and she explained:

"I do not intend to be crushed by what has happened to me, and I mean somehow, now that I am free, to begin to live."

She did not have to explain to Mr Metcalfe that looking after her father in the large, empty, dismal house with nobody to talk to, had been to all intents and purposes for a young girl a living death.

"You are quite right," he said aloud, "and somehow, in some way, you have to enjoy yourself. The first thing I think you should do is to buy yourself some new clothes. My wife always says there is nothing like a new gown to cheer oneself up."

Lady Arletta gave a little spontaneous laugh that was very attractive.

"I am sure Mrs Metcalfe is right," she said, "and that is exactly what I will do. I will go up to London as soon as I have sorted things out here, and however reprehensible it may seem, I shall buy myself some pretty gowns and because I know it would please Papa, they will not be black!"

Mr Metcalfe picked up the papers that were on the table and put them into a leather bag.

"I think, My Lady," he said, "that is the only sensible thing we have decided upon this afternoon. I promise you I shall think over your problem very carefully and hope eventually to come up with some sort of solution."

He spoke with confidence.

At the same time, at the back of his mind he knew there was really no one who was congenial, understanding and kind in her family to whom this lovely young girl could appeal for shelter.

When he said goodbye and Arletta walked with him down the long passages which led to the hall, he thought the whole house looked dismal and overwhelming, and the sooner Lady Arletta was away from it the better.

She had taken on responsibilities this last year which would have seemed heavy and arduous even to a young man, and because he was very fond of her, Mr Metcalfe wanted desperately to find some magical means by which she could be happy in the future.

'There has to be a way!' he thought as he drove away in his ancient pony-cart, drawn however by a young horse which would make short work of the five miles which lay between Weir House and the small town in which he lived and had his offices.

When he had left and Arletta saw him disappearing under the branches of the great oak trees which lined the drive, she walked back into the hall.

She was thinking, as Mr Metcalfe had done, that the house seemed dismal and even the sunlight could not percolate through the windows to light up the portraits of the Weir ancestors on the walls.

They needed cleaning, and the staircarpet, which was almost threadbare, should have been replaced years ago.

14

She was well aware that the new Earl would find it depressing and out of date.

She was quite sure that Cousin Hugo would have very strong ideas of how he could improve the house and had always thought that the sacrifices his predecessor had made to restore what had been thrown away in the past were ridiculous.

"A few debts never hurt anyone!" Arletta had heard him say once.

She was sure he had meant it as a joke.

At the same time, she was certain he did not have her father's strict principles that had made him determined he would never be in debt even for the smallest amount.

He had also been determined to make good any deficits his father had left outstanding.

She was intelligent enough to realise that this was the reaction of a man who ever since he was a small boy had known that his father was spending more than he owned and that many people and small firms suffered in consequence.

And yet now it was hard to think that the 'bad old days' might return, and she felt she could not bear after so much pinching and saving to see her Cousin Hugo being a spendthrift like her grandfather.

'I must go away,' she told herself.

Slowly she walked back through the hall where there were no servants into the room where she had been sitting with Mr Metcalfe.

It was a very pretty room because, as it faced South, there always seemed to be more sunshine in it than anywhere else, and her mother had made it particularly her own.

She had accumulated in it all the furniture that was light, pretty and mostly French, and pictures that were the opposite of the heavy portraits of the Weirs.

Winter or Summer, there were always flowers to fill the air with fragrance and make vivid patches of colour against the pale green panelling which had been installed in the reign of Queen Anne.

'I shall miss this room,' Arletta thought to herself.

Instinctively, as if she felt she would understand, she lifted her eyes to the portrait of her mother which hung over the mantelpiece.

It was a very lovely picture of a very lovely person.

Looking at it, Arletta felt that the smile on her mother's lips and the light in her eyes expressed not only her character and her personality, but also her French blood which made her so different from the Weirs, who could trace their ancestry back to Saxon times.

It seemed strange that her grandfather should have married a Frenchwoman, and yet at the same time Arletta could understand that he was a rebel like her father.

His revolt had obviously been against the pomposity of his relations, and perhaps too against the heavy propriety and gloom of the family house.

'I wish I had known my grandmother,' Arletta had often thought.

Her mother had said to her;

"You are very like her, my dearest, and when I hear you laugh, I feel like a child again and listening to my mother who always seemed to come into the Nursery laughing."

Arletta looked at the portrait for some time. Then she said aloud:

"You will have to help me, Mama, because it is going to be very difficult to know what I can do."

Then she turned away to begin thinking once again that the first real task must be to find herself a chaperon.

She had a vague idea in her mind that there were Ladies of Quality who would present a young girl not only at Court, but to the Social World.

She had no idea how one would find one, and instinctively, because she was very sensitive, she shied away

16

from pushing herself forward or saying in so many words that she wanted to be noticed.

She also had the uncomfortable feeling that such a plan would suggest that she had the possibility of marriage in mind.

But was she likely to find a husband here in the country where she had lived for so long, and where in fact there never seemed to be any eligible bachelors, or if there were, she had never met them?

'I do not want to marry,' she told herself. 'I want to live!'

Yet she was aware that in that day and age the two terms were synonymous.

Young women were brought up to get married as quickly as possible after they had left the School-Room.

Nothing else was open to them. The only alternative was to become an old maid, caring for some ill or tiresome parent, as she had done, and then to become a useful aunt to her nephews and nieces.

As she had none that position was obviously not open to her.

Once again she was back asking herself the same question.

'What can I do? What can I do?'

Then as she asked it, and it seemed as if even the pictures on the wall were saying the same thing, the door opened and somebody looked in.

Arletta turned round, stared, then gave an exclamation of astonishment.

"Jane! Is it really you?"

The newcomer who had just put her head round the door came into the room.

"I rang the bell but nobody answered," she explained. "but I thought perhaps I would find you here."

Arletta ran towards her and kissed her.

"Dear Jane, this is a surprise!" she said. "I had no idea you were at home."

"I only arrived this afternoon," Jane Turner replied, "and when I heard your father had died, I came at once to see you."

"That is kind of you."

"I am sorry," Jane Turner remarked.

"It was the best thing that could happen," Arletta replied. "His heart attacks grew more frequent, and he was in terrible pain from his gout. It was only because he was so execptionally strong that he survived as long as he did."

"Papa told me how well you looked after him," Jane said. "Oh, poor Arletta! It must have been terrible! I often thought of you."

"It was rather ghastly," Arletta admitted, "but I am so thrilled to see you again, Jane! Why have you come home?"

A smile appeared on the rather plain face of the woman to whom she was speaking, which for the moment, made her look almost pretty.

Arletta stared at her, then gave a little cry.

"Something has happened – I know it has! Jane, what is it?"

Jane Turner drew in her breath.

"You will hardly believe it, Arletta, but I am to be married!"

"How wonderful!" Arletta exclaimed. "And to whom?"

"You will never guess," Jane Turner replied. "To Simon Sutton!"

For a moment Arletta looked blank. Then she said:

"You do not mean . . it cannot be . .?"

"Yes, it is," Jane said. "You remember him when he was Papa's curate. You know he went out to Jamaica, and in eight years he has risen and risen, and because they appreciate him so much out there, he is to become a Bishop!"

"And you are to marry him!" Arletta cried. "Oh, Jane, how wonderful!"

"I never thought – I never dreamt," Jane said, "that he

18

loved me, and yet because he wrote to me almost every week and kept saying how much he missed me, I have of course – thought about – him."

The colour came into her cheeks and she looked down shyly, and Arletta put out her hand.

"Oh, Jane, it is like a fairy-tale! And he has loved you all this time!"

"Ever since he was here in Little Meldon," Jane replied. "I knew in a way he was unhappy when he left, but I did not dare to think it was because of me!"

"But it was!" Arletta insisted.

"Yes. He arrived in England two days ago and told me that now he could afford to be a married man, and he wants me to go back with him immediately to Jamaica, to be there when he is consecrated."

Arletta clasped her hands together.

"It is the most exciting thing I have ever heard! Oh, Jane, I am so happy for you, and I suppose you have come home to be married?"

"Of course. Papa has to marry us," Jane answered, "and as Simon has something to do in London, he arrives tomorrow evening."

"Dear Jane, I am so very glad that I shall be able to be at your wedding."

"There is no time to ask many other people," Jane replied, "and of course, I want you."

She looked a little shy as she asked:

"Will you be my only bridesmaid?"

"Of course I will," Arletta replied, "and I should have been very hurt if you had not asked me."

"It seems wrong for me to have one when I am so old," Jane said. "Do you realise I shall be twenty-eight in a month's time?"

"I am sure you are just the right age to be a Bishop's wife," Arletta laughed.

As if she could not help it Jane laughed too.

Arletta had known Jane ever since she was a child.

Because Jane was the Vicar's daughter she had not only come to play with Arletta in the Big House, but the Earl had persuaded the Vicar to teach his daughter many of the subjects which were beyond the scope of her Governess.

The Reverend Adolphus Turner was a Classical Scholar, and Arletta had studied History and Literature with him, while the Governess kept to the more mundane subjects.

She was taught music by one teacher and art by another, who both came to their Home.

Actually it was Jane, for whom it was planned she would be a Governess, who helped her with a great many other lessons.

Although there was such a difference in their ages, they had become very close friends, and if Arletta loved anyone outside her family, it was Jane.

She was more happy now than she could possibly say that Jane was to be married.

It had always seemed to her such a waste that anybody so sweet, kind and understanding could not, because she was not particularly pretty, attract the few local young men who might have been interested in her.

That she was now to be the wife of the Bishop of Jamaica exceeded all Arletta's hopes and excitedly she made Jane tell her exactly what had happened and what her plans were for the future.

Then Jane said, "It seems strange that everything always happens at once."

"What do you mean by that?"

"Well, I have just been offered what seemed at the time a wonderful opportunity, and actually, I had accepted it."

"What was it?" Arletta asked.

"You remember Lady Langley, to whom your mother introduced me when she wanted somebody to teach her children?"

"Yes, of course I remember."

"Well, I had just finished teaching the last one who is

going to School next term," Jane explained, "when Lady Langley begged me to go to France."

"To France!" Arletta exclaimed in surprise.

"It is a very strange story," Jane said, "but Lady Langley's brother married a French girl, the sister of the *Duc* de Sauterre. Apparently she died four years ago and although Lady Langley offered to bring up the two children the *Duc* insisted that their place was in France."

Arletta was listening intently as Jane continued;

"Because she felt rather remiss at never having visited her niece and nephew, Lady Langley went to the *Duc*'s Castle a few weeks ago."

The way Jane spoke made Arletta ask:

"What happened? What was wrong?"

"Well, quite naturally Lady Langley was horrified," Jane said, "because although David – that is her nephew – is down for Eton and will be going there in a year, he cannot speak English!"

"He will have a terrible time, if that is true," Arletta explained.

"That is what Lady Langley thinks. The little girl, who is younger, is of course in the same position, but in her case it is not so urgent."

"So you were going there to teach them?" Arletta said.

"That is what Lady Langley had arranged, and I had promised her that I would leave in what is four days from now."

"Is she very upset that you cannot go?"

"She does not know," Jane answered. "She arranged everything, then she went off with Lord Langley for a cruise in the Mediterranean. It is impossible for me to get in touch with her, and I feel dreadful, I do really, Arletta, at letting her down. At the same time, I can hardly refuse Simon, can I?"

"No, of couse not," Arletta agreed, "but I feel very sorry for the little boy . ."

She stopped suddenly.

"Jane!" she said in a strange voice.

"What is it?"

"I think I have found a solution both to your problem and to mine."

Jane just looked at her, and after a moment Arletta said:

"I will go to France in your place! It is what I have always wanted to do, and it seems as if Mama has sent you in answer to my prayers!"

Jane stared at her in sheer astonishment.

"You cannot do that!"

"Of course I can," Arletta said. "Just before you came I had Mr Metcalfe here, and I was worrying myself sick about where I could go or whom I could stay with, because Cousin Hugo, whom you will remember, has said he wants to move in as soon as possible, and I am to leave."

"Oh, Arletta, I am so sorry about that," Jane said. "It is unkind to turn you out of your home, although I suppose you would not really want to stay now."

"No, of course not," Arletta agreed. "At the same time, I cannot live alone in the Dower House, nor can I think of any relation who would be pleased to have me."

"I cannot believe that . . ." Jane began, then was silent.

She knew all Arletta's relations and had always thought secretly they were a very depressing lot.

As if Arletta could read her thoughts, she said:

"You are quite right. That is just what I have been thinking, and I am sure, Jane, that I could take your place and be you and nobody need ever know."

"It is impossible!" Jane cried.

"Why?" Arletta asked. "You said Lady Langley is away on a cruise. For how long?"

"I think at least a month, perhaps six weeks."

Arletta smiled.

"Well, there is no need for her to know what has happened until she returns. By time that I shall have seen

22

France, as I have always longed to do! If I am a success, they will keep me. If not, I can come back and perhaps move into the Dower House, and pay a companion to live with me."

Jane made a little grimace.

"That sounds pretty ghastly!"

"I know," Arletta agreed, "but it would be better than staying with one of my aunts or cousins, for you know exactly what they are like!"

Jane got up from the sofa on which they were both sitting and walked across the room.

"I am sure I am not doing the right thing in letting you go to France," she said.

"What do you mean by that?" Arletta asked.

There was a little pause as Jane was obviously choosing her words rather carefully.

Then after a moment she said;

"Lady Langley said the *Duc* was a very fierce and rather terrifying person. Actually, I am not worried about him so much as the other Frenchmen you will meet, for Arletta, you are very, very pretty!"

Arletta laughed.

"Now I know what you are thinking about, but it is very unlikely that any Frenchmen, who I have always been told are excessively proud and give themselves airs, would take notice of a mere Governess!"

Jane, knowing how innocent Arletta was, wondered how she could put into words what the Frenchmen were likely to think about a Governess who was as pretty as her friend.

Then she remembered that Lady Langley had been almost apologetic in asking her to undertake the education of her nephew and niece because the *Duc*'s Castle was in such an isolated part of the Dordogne.

There were, she had said, no companions for Pauline and David because as far as she could ascertain, there were very few neighbours in the vicinity of the Castle.

"The *Duc* spends most of his time in Paris, which is a good thing because as far as I can make out, he terrifies the whole staff of the Castle, which is a splendid example of French architecture and is kept up in a very magnificent, almost Royal manner."

She paused and knew that Arletta was listening intently before she continued:

"Lady Langley went on to say: 'I am afraid, dear Miss Turner, you will find it very dull, but I am so distressed that my nephew will suffer at Eton simply because the *Duc* has a most unfair prejudice against the English!'

" 'He has?' I asked her in surprise.

" 'He was very, very angry when my brother, Richard, married the *Duc*'s sister, and so were his father and mother. But they fell in love and to all intents and purposes eloped together. When it was too late for her parents to do anything about it, they went back and said they were sorry to have upset them, and they were forgiven. But according to reports the present *Duc* never forgave his sister.'

" 'It sounds like a novel,' I said.

" 'I suppose it does really,' Lady Langley said apologetically, 'but the children are going to suffer, and that is something I cannot allow.'

" 'So you have persuaded the *Duc* to employ an English Governess?' I answered.

" 'I can assure you he is very reluctant to do so, and says he has no wish to have an Englishwoman inside his house,' Lady Langley replied.

" 'But you managed to persuade him!'

" 'With great difficulty, and I am afraid, Miss Turner, in consequence, you will not have a very warm welcome. But will you please, and I do beg of you, almost on my knees, do this for my sake?'

"I could hear the beseeching note in the voice of the employer who had been exceedingly kind to me in the six years I had taught her children, so you can understand that after that, I could hardly say 'No'."

24

"Of course you could not," Arletta agreed, "and it would be terrible to let her down now that she is so happy to think that the boy, at any rate, will be able to speak English."

She knew Jane was hesitating, and added:

"It is a question of time as far as he is concerned, and if you refuse to teach him and do not send anybody in your place, the *Duc* will be more prejudiced against the English than he is already. David will therefore arrive at Eton speaking only French, which will be disastrous!"

"I must say," Jane said, "although my conscience was pricking me and I was feeling very uncomfortable, I never thought of finding somebody to send in my place."

"If you are now thinking of looking around for another Governess," Arletta said, "you are much mistaken! I intend to go instead of you! Honestly, dearest Jane, it is the answer I have been waiting for, and is like a sign from Heaven that I am not forgotten."

Jane gave a tender little laugh. Then she said;

"No one could ever forget you, Arletta. You are the nicest person I have ever known, and you know that Papa and I, and everybody else in the village, love you."

"Thank you," Arletta said. "If you love me, then let me do what I want to do, and that is to go to France."

She gave a cry and said;

"Just before you arrived I was looking at Mama's portrait for signs of her French blood."

"I cannot imagine anybody could look more English than your mother," Jane said glancing up at the portrait.

"That is where you are wrong," Arletta said, "for she was Norman. My grandmother came from Normandy, and Mama said all her relatives had blue eyes and fair hair."

Jane did not speak for a moment. Then she said;

"Perhaps it would please the *Duc* to know that you had French blood in your veins. On the other hand, it might make him feel that you are not such a good

25

teacher of English as you might otherwise be."

Arletta laughed.

"Now you are trying to frighten me, but I can promise you, Jane, that I am not in the least afraid of the Big Bad *Duc*! If he is too ferocious, I can always come home without a reference. To go there will not alter my future life as it would yours."

Jane put her arm around Arletta's shoulders before she said:

"If I let you go, Arletta, will you give me your solemn promise, and I mean this very seriously . . ."

"What is it?"

"That you will not listen to anything flattering or complimentary that is said to you by any Frenchman."

"Why should you say that?"

"Frenchmen are different from Englishmen," Jane said. "First of all, they are married when they are very young, as I understand the *Duc* was, according to the choice of their parents. It is not a question of love, but of convenience."

"Mama told me about that," Arletta remarked. "It sounds to me a very cold-blooded way of getting married."

"I am sure it is," Jane said, "but it is something that happens, and after that they usually have a great number of love affairs, which of course Papa would think very reprehensible."

Arletta was silent before she said;

"I do not think that is peculiar to the French. After all, even here in Little Meldon I have heard people talking of the love affairs of the Prince of Wales."

"They should not gossip to you about it," Jane said sharply.

Arletta laughed.

"You cannot shut me up in a glass case, dear Jane, even though you have always tried to keep everything unpleasant from me ever since I was a baby."

Jane smiled. Then she said:

"You were such an adorable child, just as you are adorable now. It seems wrong somehow that you should ever hear about anything unpleasant in life."

"While you can, I suppose!" Arletta laughed. "Oh, Jane, I have grown up now! I am nearly twenty and although I do live, as one might say, 'in the back of beyond', I read the newspapers and novels. It was in fact, the main recreation I had when Papa was ill and I had to look after him. My only other relaxation was when I gossiped with the servants."

Jane laughed.

"I am sure it has been a life of scintillating amusement!"

Then because she thought she had been too frivolous, she went on:

"Dearest, I know the terrible time you have had. Papa has told me about it. If it will really make you happy to go to France, as long as you promise to take the greatest care of yourself, I will agree, even though I think it is wrong for me to let you do so."

"You really will?" Arletta asked excitedly.

Her eyes were sparkling and she looked so lovely that Jane thought everybody would tell her it was crazy for anyone looking like Arletta to think of going off to France, having no idea of what might happen to her there.

"I shall have to think about it," she said.

"There is nothing to think about," Arletta said, "except how I can be you. I suppose, Jane, you have a passport?"

"As a matter of fact I had one ready," Jane said, "but now I shall not need it because Simon is arranging for me to be included on his as his wife."

"Well, that solves one problem," Arletta said. "I shall be 'Miss Jane Turner'!"

"It does not suit you."

"It suits me far better than you think," Arletta argued. "I shall be 'Miss Jane Turner, off to France to see the world'!"

"I think you are going to find it a very small one," Jane said. "Just a Castle in a very quiet, isolated part of the country with two children and a great number of servants. I doubt if there will be anybody else."

"I shall be very disappointed if I do not see the disagreeable *Duc*!"

"If you do, you must promise to look severely business-like, and make it quite clear that you are a Vicar's daughter!"

Jane paused, then she said;

"Promise me that you will always, always lock your bedroom door at night!"

Arletta stared at her for a moment. Then she went into peals of laughter.

"Oh, Jane," she said. "You have been reading far too many novelettes! I do not believe for a moment that the grand, stuck-up, proud *Duc* will condescend to notice a poor, humble little Governess, and if, as you say, he is always in Paris he is doubtless surrounded by all the beautiful, exotic women who any real Lady pretends do not exist!"

"And you are a real Lady, Arletta!" Jane said.

"But not so stupid or so half-witted as not to know that the Courtesans of Paris are the most extravagant, the most exotic, and the most seductive in the whole world!"

Jane looked at her severely.

"You should not be talking of such things, and how dare you even know of the existence of such terrible women?"

"I have read about them, heard about them, and if you want to know, occasionally Papa has talked about them!" Arletta retorted. "Really, Jane, if anyone is being a 'fuddy-duddy' with her head buried in the sand, it is you!"

Jane threw up her hands as if in dismay, and Arletta laughed.

Her laughter seemed to lighten the room as if the sunshine was suddenly flooding into it.

Chapter Two

Steaming towards Bordeaux, Arletta thought it was the most exciting thing that had ever happened to her.

She had in fact had a dozen arguments with Jane before she finally capitulated and agreed that she should go to France.

"Remember, dearest Jane," she said over and over again, "that I can come home if things do not go right, for it does not matter to me if I do not have a reference, as it would have to you."

Jane saw the logic of this.

At the same time, she was desperately afraid that Arletta, innocent and completely without knowledge of the world, would find herself in difficulties with which she would not be able to cope.

However, she was reassured by everything that Lady Langley had told her about the *Duc* de Sauterre, and also, as Arletta had said, she could come home if she wanted to.

"Anything," Arletta said fervently, "would be better than settling down in the Dower House, or being forced even for a little while to live with one of my relations."

She had discussed with Jane the possibility of her finding somebody who would chaperon her in London, and present her at Court.

Jane said at once that the person who would be best able to help her there would be Lady Langley.

"As soon as she comes back from her cruise you must talk to her about it," she said, "and I am sure as you have taken my place with her nephew and niece she will feel very grateful, and under an obligation to you."

Arletta knew that Jane was right, and that Lady Langley, who had been a friend of her mother, would certainly help.

She had been kindness itself when Reverend Turner had written to her on Jane's behalf asking her if she could recommend her as a Governess.

Lady Langley had written back by return saying she was in need of a Governess for her own children, and she was sure that anyone who had lived in their village and was known to them would be very suitable.

Jane had in fact, been a great success as Governess to Lady Langley's children, and, as she said, had been very depressed at the thought of leaving the house where she had been so happy.

Lady Langley is just like your mother," she told Arletta, "and I know that just as she looked after me, she would be only too willing to look after you."

"All I have to do," Arletta said, her eyes dancing, "is to fill in the time until Lady Langley returns from the Mediterranean, and what could be better than that I should do so teaching her nephew and niece, and at the same time seeing France, as I am longing to?"

Finally Jane was convinced and she showed Arletta the instructions she had received from the *Duc*'s secretary.

He had written in a rather stiff, ponderous English, obviously translating it, and Jane said;

"I do not know whether I should be insulted that he thinks I would not understand French."

Then she laughed.

"One thing is quite certain, that you speak French better than I do, in fact like a native."

"Which I am because of Grandmama," Arletta said.

Her mother had been so insistent that she should speak the Parisian French as spoken by the great families of France, that they had often had 'French Days' when Arletta was small, in which they spoke nothing but French, whatever they were doing.

It became a game which even her father joined in, and Arletta knew that by the time her mother died her French was perfect.

It was certainly going to come in very useful now, and as the ship carried her towards Bordeaux she practised sentences to herself and read a French novel which she had found amongst her mother's books.

The sun was shining and Bordeaux from the sea looked very impressive, despite the fact that Arletta knew it had always been a Commercial town.

Since the time of the Romans it had become a leading centre of the wine trade, and Arletta thought that her father would have been interested if he knew where she was, for it was the red wine of that area which had made him suffer so acutely in the last years of his life.

The instructions which Jane had given her told her that when the ship arrived at Bordeaux she was to take a train which would bring her to the station nearest to the *Duc*'s Castle, and there she would be met by a carriage.

Everything was very clear and the only trouble was that the Steamer had been late in leaving Plymouth Harbour, and so therefore they were late in docking.

Although if punctual she would have had several hours before catching the train, Arletta was very afraid she would miss it.

She had never before travelled by herself and she was surprised how many people offered to help her.

The porters had vied with each other to carry her baggage, several elderly women asked if there was anything she needed, and she had no idea it was because she looked so lovely and at the same time so young and helpless.

She and Jane had had a long talk over what she should wear as a Governess.

"I have not bought anything while Papa has been so ill, so everything I possess is really in rags," Arletta said.

"I must have some new gowns and I was going to buy a whole new wardrobe of clothes in London."

"You must certainly not have anything too smart," Jane said firmly, "or I am sure the *Duc* will be suspicious that you are not what you appear to be."

"At the same time, I have no wish to look like a beggar maid," Arletta replied, "and I think in what I am wearing now even the children would question my authority."

Jane thought it was not her clothes which would make them question her, but her looks, but there was no point in saying so and starting the argument all over again as to whether she should or should not go.

She therefore said:

"The best thing we can do is to go into Worcester. You can buy some clothes there that will not look too sensational or too expensive to be beyond the purse of an ordinary Governess."

They left the next morning very early so that they could be back at the Vicarage by the time Simon Sutton was due to arrive.

As Jane had known, there were some very pretty clothes in the shops of Worcester, which was a large market-town.

She had however to admit to herself that whatever Arletta put on seemed to become a perfect frame for her beauty.

She also had a way of wearing her clothes which gave her a style of her own, which Jane, without saying so, again thought was due to her French blood.

"She has *chic*," she told herself, "which is something I could never acquire."

She was very touched when Arletta insisted on buying her a dress and a coat in which to travel to Jamaica, and also a very pretty evening gown.

"It is part of my wedding present to you," she said, "and will be far more useful than a brooch or a necklace, which I would have given otherwise."

"You are not to be so extravagant!" Jane said automatically.

"If that is the repressive voice you use to your pupils, I am sorry for them!" Arletta said.

Then they were both laughing, and buying clothes seemed to make them laugh too, until they returned to the Vicarage feeling the whole day had been one of sunshine.

Simon Sutton was waiting for them, and when Arletta saw the expression in his eyes as he looked at Jane, she realised how lucky her friend was.

It did not matter to him that she was actually rather plain. He loved her, and there was no doubt that Jane was head-over-heels in love with the only man who had ever wanted to marry her.

At their marriage, which took place the following morning, Arletta was sure that the angels were joining in with the choir and singing a hymn of praise.

No bride or bridegroom ever looked more radiant than Jane and Simon when they walked down the aisle together.

Arletta had remembered at the last moment where her mother had put away the exquisite lace veil which had been worn for generations by the Weir brides.

She insisted on Jane wearing it, together with a small diamond tiara which was also a family heirloom, but which she thought privately Cousin Hugo would consider not large enough to be impressive.

The big tiaras, the necklaces, the bracelets and the brooches which had all been part of the family treasures had been sold by her father as soon as he inherited to meet her grandfather's debts.

He had kept only this one small tiara for her mother to wear on special occasions.

Although Arletta had often looked at the portraits of the previous Countesses, glittering like Christmas trees, and regretted their jewels were no longer there, her mother had merely laughed.

"I am quite happy as I am," she had said, "and I can assure you, darling, that peace of mind is a far better ornamentation than a lot of unpaid debts."

Anyway, Jane was thrilled with being lent anything so beautiful, and Arletta knew that the fact that she looked, as she put it, a 'real bride' in Simon's eyes, made her wedding even happier than it was already.

There were only a few guests to drink the health of the bride and bridegroom, and they set off to have a few days honeymoon alone before they left for Jamaica.

Jane hugged Arletta when she said goodbye and whispered:

"Promise me you will look after yourself. I shall worry about you and will pray that you will be safe."

"Of course I will be safe!" Arletta said. "If anything goes wrong I shall just tell the *Duc* what I think of him and come home. After all, if I am in any difficulty I know your father will look after me."

"Of course he will," Jane replied, "but I have not told him what you are doing."

"No one must know," Arletta said quickly, "because if they do, they will try to stop me."

Jane kissed her again, then hurried to where her husband was waiting.

Arletta went back to the Big House to write only one letter before she left three days later.

This was to Mr Metcalfe. She told him that she was going to France to stay with some friends and gave him the address of the *Duc*'s Castle, just in case it was imperative for him to get in touch with her.

She was so busy her last days at home packing up that she hardly had time to think of what lay ahead.

She knew that once she had left it might be very difficult to have anything she wanted without having to plead for it with her cousin, which she would dislike having to do.

She therefore ordered the gardeners and the other servants to move to the Dower House everything she particularly wished to keep which had belonged to her mother, and found it quite surprising what a lot there was.

There was furniture, books, and pictures, and she had forgotten that the old Housekeeper had kept all her mother's clothes carefully put away in wardrobes at the top of the house.

She used to go over them regularly in case they were eaten by moths.

Because Arletta had been so unhappy at her mother's death, and her father had begun to be ill almost before she had recovered from it, she had never given a thought to her mother's furs and the other clothes in which she had looked so lovely.

Now, although many of them were out of date, she thought that some of the things would certainly suit her and could be altered, while the furs and coats would be useful in the winter.

"Why did you not remind me that we had all these things?" she asked the Housekeeper.

"I thought it might bring back unhappy memories, M'Lady," was the answer, and there was no reply to that.

In fact, because they brought back memories of happier days, Arletta put some of the things that had belonged to her mother into the luggage she was taking with her to France.

There were some beautiful nightgowns, and to wear over them there was a négligée of blue satin that was far more attractive than the plain wool of the dressing-gown that Arletta had worn since she was sixteen.

'No one will see me,' she told herself, 'so I shall look glamorous when I am alone at night, and what could be more appropriate in a Castle?'

However much Jane had disparaged the *Duc* by repeating what Lady Langley had told her, Arletta could not help thinking it was rather like living in a fairy-tale.

She was going to an enchanted Castle in France in a part that she knew from her books was famous for its ancient Castles.

She wished she had had more time to read about the

Dordogne where the *Duc*'s family had lived for centuries.

Of course, when she wanted them she could not find any books about that particular part of France, and thought the first thing she would do when she had time was to try to find Guide Books which would tell her all she wished to know.

When she reached Bordeaux she found herself thrilled and delighted with the people she could see in the streets because they looked so different from anyone in England.

The ordinary peasants with their full skirts and shawls over their heads had a charm of their own, as had the Nuns with their varying head-dresses.

There was also occasionally a glimpse of women dressed in the strange lace cap and lace-trimmed apron that was characteristic of the district, and even the *Gendarmes* in their smart uniform looked as if they had stepped straight out of an Opera or a Musical Comedy.

There was however little time to look round on her way to the station, and she actually caught the train with only fifteen minutes to spare.

She watched from the windows the undulating country-side, the huge woods that seemd to her like dragon forests, and the occasional glimpse on the top of a hill of an ancient Château or Castle.

This, Arletta told herself, was Fairyland as she had always wanted to see it.

Her first glimpse of the *Duc*'s Castle was exactly what she had hoped it would be.

Silhouetted against the sky, it looked very impressive, very formidable and, although she would hate to admit it, rather frightening.

In the distance the windows seemed little more than arrow slits, and the crenellated tops of some of the towers reminded her of the soldiers who must have once guarded the Castle and been ready to repel the enemy from whatever direction they came.

Beneath the Castle was a river, and a stone wall rose

straight above the bank on one side to where the building itself began.

Arletta found herself thinking of bleak dungeons in which prisoners were incarcerated in damp darkness until they died, and as they drew nearer she had the uncomfortable feeling that eyes were watching her from the narrow windows.

Then as the carriage which had met her at the station crossed a bridge and passed the Castle, she realised they were approaching it from the East side, moving up a narrow roadway with cottages on either side of it.

Almost at the top was a very ancient Church which Arletta was certain was Twelfth Century, like the Castle.

Then there was a double gate in the centre of the great wall which led into the Castle itself.

She drew in her breath as they drove into a great courtyard, at the far end of which there was an impressive entrance to the house. This was up a large number of steps with an arched doorway romantically curved and yet, at the same time, severe and again somewhat foreboding.

The carriage, which was drawn by four horses, came to a standstill and a footman wearing an elaborate claret-coloured livery trimmed with gold braid ran down the steps to open the door.

Arletta stepped out and she thought he looked at her in surprise.

Then at the top of the stairs there was an even more impressive figure who she guessed was the Major Domo.

"You are *M'mselle* Turner?" he asked in French.

"Yes, that is right," Arletta agreed.

"Please come this way, *M'mselle*."

He led her through what she felt was an extremely impressive mediaeval Hall with a huge open fireplace which could easily burn a whole tree in the winter.

There were ancient flags hanging on either side of it, but she only had a quick glimpse before the Major Domo escorted her down a long passage.

She wondered where she was being taken until he opened the door of what she guessed immediately was the office of the secretary, saying as he did so:

"*M'mselle* Turner has arrived, *Monsieur!*"

A middle-aged man with greying hair rose slowly from a desk, and Arletta knew this would be *Monsieur* Byien who had written to Jane and given her instructions for the journey.

He held out his hand; then as he looked at Arletta the smile on his lips seemed suddenly frozen and he stared at her in astonishment.

"You are *Mademoiselle* Turner?" It was a question.

"I must thank you, *Monsieur*," Arletta said in her perfect French, "for the excellent directions you gave me for my journey. The Steamship was a little late arriving at Bordeaux and I was afraid I might miss the connecting train, but as you can see I am here!"

"Will you sit down, *Mademoiselle*?"

Monsieur Byien indicated a chair in front of the desk and Arletta sat down, wondering if perhaps she should have worn spectacles to make herself look older.

She had in fact, considered it, then thought it seemed a theatrical gesture which she might regret.

Also she was quite certain that sooner or later she would forget the spectacles and everybody would be aware that she could see without them.

Instead she had arranged her hair in a very plain and what she hoped was an unattractive manner, and wore a bonnet which had belonged to her mother and was far too old for her.

Her efforts had obviously not been very effective because *Monsieur* Byien said:

"I understood from Lady Langley, *Mademoiselle*, that you were very much older than you look."

"I have always been told, *Monsieur*, that it is very rude for a gentleman to discuss a lady's age," Arletta replied, "and if I look young, which I take as a compliment, it is something which I assure you will be remedied by time."

Monsieur Byien smiled and it swept what Arletta realised now was a look of anxiety from his lined face.

"That is indisputable, *Mademoiselle*," he said. "At the same time, you must forgive me when I say I was not expecting an English Governess to look like you."

"Let me assure you, *Monsieur*," Arletta said, "that I am a very good teacher of English, which I understand is why I am wanted here. I cannot believe my looks, one way or another, will effect my proficiency in my own language."

"English may be your own language, *Mademoiselle*," *Monsieur* Byien said, "but I must compliment you on your French."

"Thank you," Arletta replied, "and if you think my French is good, I assure you that my English is very much better!"

"Then, as you say, that is all that matters," *Monsieur* Byien replied.

But again he looked worried and Arletta was aware there was something about her appearance which he did not mention, but was certainly, from his point of view, a distinct disadvantage.

He rose to his feet.

"I am sure, *Mademoiselle*, you would like to see your rooms and meet your charges, and I feel sure they are looking forward to meeting you."

He led Arletta from his office for what seemed a long walk along the ground floor of the Castle.

It certainly was impressive, the furniture naturally being of a much later date than the Castle itself.

There was, because the windows were so small, little light, and Arletta had the idea that in the winter, and when it was dark, the shadows would be oppressive and rather frightening.

They climbed a staircase, which was obviously not the main one of the Castle, to the next floor and as they entered the room at the top of it, Arletta realised they were in one of the round towers.

The room was a Sitting-Room, or rather, she guessed, the School-Room, and there were two children in it.

The boy was arranging a number of toy soldiers, that were skilfully made of wood and painted, on a table.

The small girl was watching him, holding a doll in her arms as she did so.

They both looked up as *Monsieur* Byien entered and their eyes went from him to Arletta.

"*Mademoiselle* Turner has arrived," he said in French, "and I know you have been looking forward to meeting her."

He walked to the table saying:

"This, *Mademoiselle*, is David, who as you see has a fine collection of soldiers, and this is Pauline."

Arletta held out her hand.

"I am delighted to meet you, David," she said, "and I hope you will show me your soldiers. My father had a collection of which he was very proud."

She was just about to say that when they were set out they depicted the Battle of Waterloo, when she realised that that would be somewhat tactless in a French household. She turned instead towards Pauline.

The little girl had curly chestnut hair falling on either side of a very sweet, pretty face which seemed filled with two large eyes.

"Have we got to do lots and lots of lessons, *Mademoiselle*?" she asked.

"I hope not," Arletta replied, "but I certainly want you to tell me all about this magnificent Castle, and since I want to learn about it that will be a lesson for me."

The two children looked at her in surprise, then *Monsieur* Byien said:

"Your rooms, *Mademoiselle*, like the children's, are on the floor above, and when you are ready I am sure Pauline will show you the way upstairs."

"Thank you," Arletta replied.

He looked at her again, she thought, with a worried expression on his face before he went from the School-Room, shutting the door behind him.

Arletta slipped off her travelling-cape which had made her feel rather hot for the last part of the journey, untied the ribbons on her bonnet, and put them down on a chair by the door.

Then she said:

"I expect you know that I have come here to teach you English, but you must tell me how it would be best for me to do so, because you, David, have to learn very quickly."

David looked down at the soldiers he was holding in his hand and said:

"I want to learn English, then I can go to England and never come back here again!"

He spoke violently, then looked over his shoulder towards the door as if afraid he had been overheard.

Arletta was surprised. Then she said:

"Are you saying you do not like living here at the Castle?"

David was silent for a moment; then as if he saw no reason why he should not tell the truth, he said:

"I hate it! I am English, I am not French! They are our enemies!"

As he spoke he gave another quick look over his shoulder and Arletta said:

"They are not our enemies now. England is friendly with France, but of course you are English. Have you ever been there?"

David shook his head.

"No, but *mon Père* used to talk about England and he told me that one day I would live there, but Uncle Etienne wants me to stay here."

He lowered his voice before he went on:

"He is hoping I shall be sent away from Eton as soon as I get there. But if I cannot stay there, I shall run away and hide somewhere in England so that I shall not have to come back to France."

The way he spoke told Arletta that here was a problem she had not expected.

Then, just as she was wondering what she should say, the door opened and a servant appeared carrying a tray.

"The Chef's compliments, *M'mselle*, and he has ordered you English tea. We do not have such a thing in the Castle, but he said being English you would expect it."

"Thank you very much!" Arletta replied. "After a long journey a cup of tea is what I would really enjoy."

The servant put the tray down on a table and she saw it contained a pot of tea, a cup and two plates, one filled with sandwiches, the other with little *pâtisseries* filled with cream that only the French could make so skilfully.

As soon as the servant had left the room both the children ran towards the table to stare at the tea with curiosity.

"I remember my father having tea like that," David said, "but we are not allowed tea here. We have to be French and drink coffee or wine."

"I expect you would like to share my tea with me." Arletta said. "Suppose you both start with a sandwich?"

The children ate most of the sandwiches and also enjoyed the *pâtisseries*.

Pauline said very little until, licking the cream from her fingers, she asked:

"When David goes to School in England, may I come and live with you?"

"When David goes to England you will live with your aunt," Arletta said. "I feel sure she would like to have you."

"Uncle Etienne hates her!" Pauline replied. "So if I am to live in England, I will have to hide somewhere where he will never find me!"

Arletta could not say this was untrue, and she therefore said after a long pause:

"You will have to tell me why your uncle hates England so much."

"He hates everybody and everything," David said, "but we are too frightened of him to say so."

"It would be very rude if you did, as you are living in his house!" Arletta remarked.

"He hates us!" David said in a low, conspiratorial voice. "But rather than let us go, Uncle Etienne would shut us up in the dungeons!"

The way he spoke made Arletta laugh.

"I am sure that is not true," she said. "Nobody is shut up in dungeons these days."

"Uncle Etienne would use them, if he could," David insisted. "I will show them to you and you will see the bones of the prisoners who died there."

Arletta shuddered.

"I have no wish to do that. Now, suppose you both show me my Bedroom and where you sleep?"

There was a twisting stone staircase on one side of the tower only just wide enough, Arletta thought, for the servants to carry her trunks up to her room.

As she reached it she felt very high up in the air and isolated almost from the world.

The children had two rooms, each occupying half of the floor above the School-Room, and she was on the floor above them.

Her Bedroom had windows on each side which gave her a magnificent view of the surrounding countryside, and the room itself had a very high ceiling with ancient beams that were carved, the space between them being painted red.

The carpet was the same colour and so were the short curtains over the windows.

Above her bed was a strange heraldic design and David explained:

"This was the room used by one of Uncle Etienne's ancestors who fought against the British and killed twenty men before he himself was struck down."

There was a little pause before he added, almost as if he felt as if he should not do so;

"The servants say he haunts the whole tower, but actually the Castle is full of ghosts!"

"Is it really?" Arletta asked. "Have you ever seen them yourself?"

"*I* have!" Pauline chimed in. "I have seen lots and lots of ghosts, and although the servants run away and scream, I am very brave! I just say a little prayer, like Mama taught me to do, and they disappear."

"I expect they were only just shadows," David said scornfully. "The real ghosts in the Castle are not what you see, but what you hear: prisoners groaning, the wounded crying out in pain, and the shrieks of those being stabbed to death!"

He spoke so dramatically that Arletta gave a cry.

"You are not to frighten me," she said. "And I am sure if you talk like that it will frighten your sister."

David shrugged his shoulders in a gesture that was typically French.

"We have to put up with it, whatever we feel," he said. "If you want the truth, *Mademoiselle*, I do not believe we will ever escape and be able to get to England."

"That is nonsense!" Arletta said quickly. "In a year's time you are going to Eton, which as you know, is the best School in England, and that is why your uncle has been persuaded by your aunt, Lady Langley, to let me come here to teach you English."

She paused to add impressively:

"But you will have to work hard, because you would hate being the only boy in the School unable to speak to all the others. So the sooner we start, the better."

"I want to learn," David said, "not because I am going to Eton, for I am quite certain that Uncle Etienne will stop me from doing that, but so that I can escape. I have . . ."

44

He had started to say something, then he stopped as if he thought it would be indiscreet to tell her his secrets, and walked away abruptly to look out through the window.

Arletta looked round and saw that the servants had brought up her trunks and opened them for her, and while she was wondering if she should unpack and perhaps ask the children to help her, a maidservant in a mob-cap came into the room and bobbed a small curtsy.

"The Housekeeper says I'm to unpack for you, *M'mselle.*"

"That would be very kind," Arletta replied. "I hope there will be room for all my clothes."

"I'll find room," the maidservant replied.

Arletta looked at the watch which had belonged to her mother and which were pinned on her blouse.

"It is nearly six o'clock," she said. "You just tell me what to do, and at what time you go to bed."

"We have dinner downstairs in the Dining-Room at seven o'clock," David answered.

"In the Dining-Room?" Arletta repeated in surprise.

"Uncle Etienne said French families eat together and children eat at the same time as their parents. It is only the English who send their children to bed because they do not like the sight of them!"

"That is not true!" Arletta said quickly. "English children are sent to bed early because being so young they need more sleep than grown-ups."

"Uncle Etienne says only the French behave with affection to all their relations, from grandparents down to the youngest child. But English children are shut away in the Nursery or in the School-Room until they are grown up, because their parents and everybody else thinks they are bores."

There was some truth in this, Arletta had to admit, but she thought it was extremely unfair of the *Duc* to use it as a weapon to try to put his nephew and niece against their father's people.

Aloud she said:

"I have lots of arguments in defence of the English, but as I am rather tired I think I would like now to wash and change my gown, and I will join you later. Then you can show me where we have dinner."

"Very well," David agreed. "We will say *au revoir*, *Mademoiselle*."

He bowed to her in what Arletta knew was a very French fashion, and Pauline dropped her a small curtsy.

Then the two children went from the room, and she said to the housemaid, "Will you show me where I can wash? And I would like, if possible, to have a bath."

"A bath, *M'mselle*?" the housemaid exclaimed. "That's very English! But if you want one, I'll order it to be brought upstairs."

Arletta did not protest, as she had a feeling any ordinary Governess might have done.

Laboriously, first a hip-bath was brought to her bedroom and then a manservant carried up several cans of hot water, which were brought into the room by the maid.

There was, she discovered, behind a curtain at one side of her room, a basin but no bath.

She thought the *Duc* would be extremely annoyed if he knew how often she was going to ask for a bath to be brought upstairs, unless he expressly forbade it.

But she could not believe that in such a huge Castle he could really be aware of everything that happened.

And yet quite obviously from the way the children spoke he overshadowed their lives and, she was quite certain, everybody else's, including *Monsieur* Byien's.

It was all rather fascinating and while she soaked away what she thought of as 'travel stains' in the hip-bath, she found herself vastly intrigued by everything she had seen so far.

At the same time, she was aware that she was going to have a difficult time erasing from the children's minds everything the *Duc* had deliberately implanted against their father's country.

Dinner was a formal meal which, for a Governess and two small children, she found incredible.

Waited on by a Butler and three footmen, they sat in the huge Baronial Dining-Room which could have accommodated nearly a hundred people.

The *Duc*'s chair at the far end of the table, carved and painted with the arms of the Sauterre family, looked like a throne.

They sat in what were their proper places at the far end of the table, and as course followed course of delicious food, Arletta, who was hungry, enjoyed every mouthful, although she was aware that by the end of the meal Pauline was half-asleep.

David however ate heartily and chatted away answering her questions about the Castle.

He had obviously, she thought, been indoctrinated with the importance of the Sauterre family to the exclusion of a great deal of French history which might have been more useful to him.

As for the English, they were obviously the enemy.

"Uncle Etienne's ancestors were at the Field of the Cloth of Gold," David announced. "And they fought to try to save St Joan of Arc who was burnt to death by the English, although she was a Saint!"

"All that happened a long time ago," Arletta said firmly.

"The English may have won the Battle of Waterloo," David said, "but Uncle Etienne says they were very cruel to Napoleon when he was a prisoner on the Isle of St Helena."

"I think what you have to do," Arletta said eventually, "is to learn a little about the English before you come to England. Do not forget, David, that you belong to an ancient and very distinguished family. In fact, the Redruths were Chieftains or perhaps Kings in Cornwall long before Willam the Conqueror invaded us from Normandy!"

Jane had told her this, but she had not realised at the time how important it was going to be.

"He was French, and he won!" David said.

"But now the English Empire spreads over half the world," Arletta said, "and I think you must learn about that."

She sighed before she said:

"Actually, you are very, very lucky."

"Why?" David asked in a somewhat hostile tone.

"Because you are both English and French, and you therefore must try to understand both countries and do your best to keep them at peace with each other."

David looked surprised and Arletta said:

"Some of the Redruths have been Statesmen and Diplomats. You must learn about them, and how they managed to prevent war and create friendship between nations who previously had always loathed each other."

She was not sure this was true, but David would not be able to contradict her!

"Do you think war is wrong, *Mademoiselle*?" he asked.

"I think it is horrible, wicked and cruel and many men lose in war the most precious thing any of us can possess, which is life!"

David thought this over for a moment, then he said:

"Suppose they do not mind dying?"

"Everybody minds dying, especially when they are young," Arletta answered. "Life is exciting, an adventure. There is so much to do, so much to learn, so much to enjoy."

She saw David was listening and asked:

"Why should one lose something so precious, just because of some Political quarrel, or because the Ruler of one country is greedy and wants to take away what another Ruler owns?"

She thought as she spoke that this was something she must enlarge upon, and perhaps describe better than she was doing at the moment.

48

It was obvious David was impressed, and after a moment he said:

"Uncle Etienne wants me to go into the French Army!"

Without thinking, Arletta replied:

"But of course you cannot do that! I know your father would be horrified if he knew you were fighting against your own kith and kin in another country."

She spoke so violently that David stared at her.

Then she felt perhaps she had been over-emotional about something that was so much a part of her own upbringing that she could hardly believe she was listening to an English boy saying the things David had just said to her.

She cried quickly:

"I think if you have finished, we should go upstairs. I am sure Pauline wants to go to bed."

"I'se tired," Pauline said.

"Yes, of course you are," Arletta said. "Who puts you to bed? Shall I do that?"

"No, it is *ma Bonne*," Pauline said. "I want her! I want *ma Bonne*!"

Waiting outside the Dining-Room door was a middle-aged gentle-faced Frenchwoman who swept Pauline up into her arms.

"*La petite* grows very tired, *M'mselle*," she explained to Arletta. "She is not strong and should have plenty of sleep, but *Monsieur* insists the children dine downstairs and with you arriving she did not have a rest before dinner."

"Then that is something we must prevent another time," Arletta said.

"I'se tired – I'se very tired," Pauline whimpered.

The Frenchwoman carried her away and Arletta said:

"Are you ready to go to bed, too David?"

"Not yet," he said.

"Then perhaps you will show me a little of the Castle, or is it too late?"

David grinned.

"No one can stop us now that Uncle Etienne is away," he said, "and I would like to show it to you."

"Very well," Arletta said. "Let us see as much as we can before it gets too dark."

It was impossible, she realised, to see everything.

The Castle seemed to extend for miles, and there were three towers similar to that which the children used, as well as enormous Reception-Rooms in the centre block, which looked out, she discovered, over the most entrancing formal gardens.

There were pools ornamented with ancient urns, and a huge fountain sculpted with cupids and dolphins which flung water like a thousand iridescent rainbows high into the sky.

It was so lovely, and at the same time traditional and formal, very unlike the gardens at Weir House with which Arletta was so familiar.

Everything seemed to have its place, and she thought it impossible even for one revolutionary weed to raise up its head between the paved walks or the tightly clipped box-hedges.

She was not surprised to find that everything in the Castle was very luxurious.

As she had seen when she arrived, the furnishing was predominately Louis XIV and she wondered how so much had escaped the Revolution until David explained:

"Uncle Etienne says that in the Revolution most of the great treasures were hidden in a safe place like the caverns in the mountains or dungeons to which nobody could find an entrance."

In fact, the Castle had not been ransacked in the same way as those nearer to Paris.

"As it is so isolated here," David went on, "there were not many people to revolt against the reigning *Duc* of the time."

"He was very lucky," Arletta said.

David shrugged his shoulders.

"It has made Uncle Etienne more puffed up with pride than he would be otherwise. I heard one of the servants say once that he thinks he is God!"

Arletta gave a little exclamation.

"I am sure, David, you should not say such things about your uncle."

"Why not to you?" David asked. "You are the enemy, who has been forced upon him, and he already hates you before he has even met you!"

Arletta was startled.

"Do you really mean that?"

"He said to us when Aunt Margaret had left, 'Your Aunt has forced upon me against my will an English Governess, who will teach you the barbaric language which you David have to assimilate before you suffer hell in what the English call a "Public School"!' "

"That is not true!" Arletta exclaimed. "I am sure your father loved being at Eton, and all the family who have been there are very proud and very fond of their old School. They would be shocked and horrified to think you thought of it like that."

"I am prepared to go to hell, or anywhere else, as long as it is a long way from here!" David replied.

They were in the Library as he spoke, and looking at the thousands of books in the enormous room Arletta thought it strange that any child should not be intrigued by living in such a fine Castle with so much to occupy and entertain him.

She sat down on a stool in front of the empty fireplace and said:

"Tell me, David, why do you hate living here?"

For a moment he looked over his shoulder in the same surreptitious way he had done before, to make certain there was nobody near them.

Then he came closer to her as he said:

"It is horrible! I could just bear it when Mama was

alive, but now it is worse than any prison could possibly be!"

"But why? Why do you say that?" Arletta asked.

David hesitated and she wondered if he would tell her the truth. Then he said:

"It is Uncle Etienne! He hates us because Papa was English, and the whole Castle is horrible!"

He lowered his voice before he added:

"And Uncle Etienne is a murderer! He has killed two women!"

Chapter Three

Arletta, standing at the window of her Tower Bedroom, thought that on the whole it had been an extraordinary but very good day.

First, she had been delighted to find that David was not so ignorant where English was concerned as she had been led to believe.

His father had died when he was six, but until then he had talked to him in English, and only after that when his mother had brought the children to the Castle had that language been barred.

But once he had began to talk with her, the words came back even if the grammar was rather hazy, and as he was very anxious to learn she thought that in one day they had made a surprising amount of progress.

She insisted on teaching David alone, and then tried very gently to interest Pauline in the English names for flowers, food and other things around her.

The little girl tried hard, but it was obviously very much more difficult for her, and Arletta thought it was more important to get David ready for his English School.

There were so many small things too that had to be corrected: the way he wrote out his sums in arithmetic, the manner in which he addressed people, which was entirely French and would, she knew, be laughed at in England.

It was all going to take time, but she found that she was not only extremely interested in what she was doing but, she had to admit, very curious.

When David had told her last night that his uncle had

murdered two women, she had thought at first it was some kind of joke, then that the boy was lying for the sake of shocking her.

Finally she knew that this was a puzzle that she had to unravel, but it could not be done in a few minutes.

She therefore talked of other things until they both went up to bed.

In the morning what he had said was vividly in her mind, and she found herself wondering how any child could have such an idea about his uncle.

If that was what he believed, she could understand that he found it hard in the circumstances to live happily in the Castle.

After she had finished her lesson with David they went out and continued talking in English as he showed her first the formal gardens, then took her to the stables.

She had expected the *Duc*'s horses would be exceptional, as she had noticed the fine team which had met her at the station.

But she was not prepared for row upon row of stables filled with Arab-bred horses of a superb pedigree that were better than any she had seen in the whole of her life.

"Uncle Etienne has his racing-stables at Chantilly," David explained, "but these he rides himself, and of course we are allowed to ride them too."

Arletta's eyes lit up and she asked:

"Do you suppose I might ride with you?"

"Of course, if you want to," David replied, "but I did not imagine an English Governess would be keen on riding."

Then he laughed and added:

"But then you are not the sort of English Governess I was expecting."

"What did the *Duc* say?" Arletta asked.

"He said you would be prim, ugly and very strict," he replied.

54

Arletta was not certain if he was being truthful, or merely teasing her.

They arranged to ride after luncheon, but Pauline said she would rather stay with her nurse, and therefore David and Arletta rode alone.

He took her over the beautiful countryside and into one of the thick woods that she had thought of as dragon forests.

She was not surprised to find that the trees were planted with rides between them which not only facilitated riding but also shooting, and they were carefully looked after by woodcutters who were working in one of the woods they visited.

By the time they returned home she was certain that the *Duc* ran his estates very efficiently. But one little episode had upset her.

They had stopped to speak to the men who were working in a small vine-field, and the Overseer, who obviously knew David, came up to speak to them.

"Nice to see you here, *Monsieur!*" he said politely, and looked at Arletta curiously.

"This is Pierre Beauvais, *Mademoiselle*," David explained. "He looks after all Uncle Etienne's vines, and makes the most delicious wine."

Arletta held out her hand.

"I have come to the Castle," she said in French, "to teach *le petit Monsieur et Mademoiselle* Pauline English."

Pierre Beauvais looked at her in astonishment.

"You are a Governess, *M'mselle?*"

Arletta nodded.

Then as David moved away to speak to one of the other men working on the vines he said in a low voice:

"*C'est impossible!* You should go home, *M'mselle*, you will not be happy here."

"Why do you say that?" Arletta asked.

Pierre Beauvais glanced round, and she thought he was embarrassed that he had said too much.

Then as David came back he said quickly:

"Go home, *M'mselle*, it will be better for you!"

There was no chance to say any more, and driving back to the Castle Arletta thought it was a very strange conversation to have had with one of the *Duc*'s employees.

Pauline was waiting for them, and they went not into the School-Room but into the Library.

Arletta was determined to find picture-books for the little girl which would make it more interesting for her to learn English when she saw the words pictured.

There were however so many thousands of books covering the walls that it was difficult to know where to begin to look, and there seemed to be no catalogue.

Then, as the children were helping her to search, the door opened and a man came into the Library. She looked at him in surprise.

He was young, good-looking, and extremely elegantly dressed.

She was wondering who it could be when David said in a rather offhand manner:

"Oh, hello, Cousin Jacques! I did not know you were coming back today!"

"I am back," the newcomer said, "and I understand we have a visitor."

Arletta walked towards him.

"I am Jane Turner, *Monsieur*," she said, wondering as she spoke how he fitted into the organisation of the Castle.

"You are the Governess?"

There was no doubt of the astonishment in his voice and on his face, and Arletta thought what a fuss people made about her appearance.

"I gather," she said a little coldly, "that you were not expecting to find me here."

"I was expecting to find an English Governess, but not somebody who looks like you!"

"I find it difficult, *Monsieur*," Arletta said, "to understand what my looks have to do with it. The only reason I am here is to teach."

"Perhaps I should introduce myself," the young man said. "I am Jacques de Sauterre – *Comte* Jacques if you wish to be formal. I am a cousin of the *Duc*, and when I am not in Paris, I live here in the Castle."

Arletta smiled.

"I only arrived yesterday, so you will understand, *Monsieur le Comte*, that I am finding it difficult to understand the complexities of the household."

"That is not surprising," the *Comte* agreed, "and I suppose the children have not enlightened you. They are tiresome little monsters unless you bully them!"

He seemed to speak jokingly, but to Arletta's surprise David scowled at him, and Pauline, who had only glanced up when he came into the room, now had her back to him, looking through the book which she had taken down from one of the shelves.

"As you see, we are one big happy family!" the *Comte* said sarcastically, then added: "I suppose, as you have only just arrived, that you have not yet seen the *Duchesse*."

"The *Duchesse*?" Arletta gasped.

It had never occured to her that there might be another woman in the Castle.

"The *Duc*'s grandmother," the *Comte* explained. "She is very old and in bad health, and she seldoms bothers with visitors unless, of course, she is curious about them."

He looked at Arletta in a manner which was slightly insulting. Then he said:

"But I am sure, Miss Turner, she will be very, very curious about you!"

There was something in the way he spoke which made Arletta stiffen and she replied:

"You must excuse me, but I am busy trying to find a book which will interest Pauline."

"If you are expecting to find any books in English here, you are much mistaken," the *Comte* said.

"I was not expecting anything of the sort," Arletta answered, "but I cannot find a catalogue, and it is therefore difficult to know what is available."

"There must be a catalogue somewhere," the *Comte* said. "I cannot believe that my most efficient and most estimable cousin would not have everything that concerns him in perfect order!"

There was a sarcastic and rather nasty note in his voice, and Arletta merely walked towards Pauline and looked down at the book the child held in her hand.

"Shall we take that upstairs with us?" she asked.

"No, it's very dull," Pauline replied. "I want a book with lots of birds and flowers in it, or else pictures of England."

The *Comte* laughed.

"That is something you will certainly not find here, and if your uncle hears you asking for such a thing he will be very angry!"

Pauline ignored him and looked up at Arletta to say:

"Find me one, *Mademoiselle*."

"I will do my best," Arletta answered, "but it is rather difficult to know where to begin."

She tried to ignore the *Comte*, who was standing near her and looking at her in a way which she considered impertinent.

Then as if he had made up his mind he said:

"I would like to have a word with you, *Mademoiselle*. Will you come to the other end of the room?"

Arletta hesitated.

She wanted to say that she had nothing to talk to him about, then she thought that would be rude, and it would be a mistake not to be polite to one of the *Duc*'s relations.

Reluctantly, telling David to go on looking for what they required and speaking to him in English, she walked to the end of the Library where, by the huge carved fireplace, there was a sofa and several chairs.

She sat down on the sofa, then thought she had made a mistake as the *Comte* sat beside her a little closer than she considered necessary.

Lowering his voice he said:

"You have made a great mistake in coming here!"

"A mistake?" Arletta asked.

"You will find it very boring, and there are many other places in France which will amuse you, and where with your very pretty face you would be a great success."

"I do not know what you are talking about, *Monsieur*," Arletta said. "I came here to teach English to the children, who are the nephew and niece of my friend, Lady Langley, and that is what I intend to do."

"Then if you insist, you must let me help you," the *Comte* said. "It will not be easy for you to cope with the *Duc*, and as he has already made up his mind to hate you, you will find the Castle very uncomfortable when he returns."

"I am sure you mean to be kind, *Monsieur*," Arletta replied, "but I am quite prepared to 'cross my bridges when I come to them'. Since the *Duc* is not yet here, I shall do my best until he does return."

"Your best is certainly good enough for me!" the *Comte* said. "As I have already told you, I will look after you, help and guide you."

Arletta got to her feet.

"Thank you for being very kind," she said, "but to be quite honest, being English, I am quite capable of looking after myself."

She walked away from him and he did not attempt to stop her.

She heard him laugh softly and thought he was undoubtedly the sort of Frenchman Jane had warned her about.

At the same time she did not like him and she thought he might make things difficult instead of, as he had offered, helping her.

To her relief, when she reached the other end of the Library where the children were, she found he had left them and as soon as she had found several books she thought might be useful, they went upstairs to the School-Room.

As soon as they were back David said, "I do not like Cousin Jacques."

"Nor do I," Pauline chimed in, not wishing to be left out.

"Why?" Arletta asked.

She noticed that David once again looked over his shoulder, as if he was afraid of being overheard. Then he said:

"There is something about him which makes me feel uncomfortable. I do not know why."

He looked a little puzzled. Then he said:

"Mama said that we should send out waves of kindness to people so that they like us, but the waves coming from Cousin Jacques are not kind."

That was what Arletta had thought herself, but she was surprised that such a small boy should be so perceptive.

Then she thought that living in the Castle in such strange conditions had perhaps made him different from other boys.

She was afraid that if this was so he might find School in England even more difficult.

"I suppose if we all behaved properly, we would try to like everybody," she said lightly. "Although it is not always possible, at least we can make the best of them."

David was not attending. Instead he was playing with his soldiers which were on the table where he had arranged them the previous night.

"They are a very fine collection!" Arletta said. "Who gave them to you?"

"Uncle Etienne," David said. "He had them made for me, and I think his idea when he did so was not to please me, but to make me interested in becoming a soldier myself in the French Army!"

Again Arletta was aware that it was an unusual thought for a boy of eleven.

She wondered whether it was something she should try to encourage or suppress.

What would Jane have done about it in her place?

She knew Jane was very 'down-to-earth'. As her father would have said, she 'had her feet planted firmly on the ground', and except where Simon Sutton was concerned, her head was full of facts, not fantasies.

Arletta was sure that she would have faced even the Castle itself in a practical, straightforward manner.

She knew by the end of the day that for her the Castle held a magic that was inescapable, apart from being in so many ways menacing and oppressive.

She had found out that part of the main building was of a later date than the towers.

Here the windows were high and the rooms with their tapestries, pictures, and huge crystal chandeliers were so beautiful that she felt it impossible not to feel when she entered them that she walked into a fairy-tale.

To the children it was all so familiar that they were not interested, and preferred to take her to the Armoury where ancient weapons that had been used by the Sauterres over the generations were arranged on the walls.

In the centre of the room was a cannon with its round iron balls piled beside it.

They also wanted to show her the dungeons, but even David realised it had grown too dark, and it would be better if they went earlier in the day.

Just before dinner, when the children had gone to their own rooms to change and Arletta was just about to go up the stone steps to her Bedroom, a footman came to the door to say:

"*Madame la Duchesse* wishes to see you, *M'mselle*!"

Following him, Arletta felt excited at the idea of meeting the *Duc*'s grandmother.

She wondered if in any way she would be like her own grandmother, whom she could vaguely remember coming to stay with them many years ago before her father came into the title and they had moved into the family mansion.

She had thought that her grandmother was exquisite with her white hair, her delicate features, and her long thin hands.

She had been very dignified and sat as if her back was supported by a ramrod. But her eyes had often twinkled with amusement, and her laughter was very soft and melodious.

"I wish she had not died when I was so young," Arletta had often said later.

She thought now that *Madame la Duchesse* might be something like her *grandmère* after whom Arletta was named.

The footman led her a long way, in fact to the other end of the Castle, which Arletta had not yet been able to explore.

Then they went up a rather fine staircase to the First Floor, where there was an elderly maid waiting for them.

"Good evening, *M'selle*," she said politely, and then to the footman, "You must wait, Jean, to take *M'mselle* back. She'll never find her own way."

"Yes, that is true," Arletta said. "Please wait, or I shall be completely lost."

She then followed the maid through a beautifully painted door into a small hall out of which opened two other doors.

In the next moment she found herself in the *Duchesse*'s Bedroom.

It was different from any room she had seen before. There was a huge bed on a dais with curtains falling behind it from a corolla fixed to the ceiling.

Propped up against a number of pillows was the strangest old lady Arletta had ever seen.

She was very old. Her face, which might once have been beautiful, was wrinkled and lined like Chinese parchment.

Her hair was white, but so skilfully arranged that Arletta suspected it to be a wig.

Round her neck she wore a dozen ropes of huge pearls, and glittering in her ears were diamond ear-rings which swung and glittered with every movement she made.

Her hands, which were blue-veined, were weighed down with rings and there were half a dozen bracelets on each of her wrists.

Although it was summer, her bed was covered with an ermine bedspread which was growing slightly yellow in colour.

As Arletta moved nearer to the bed she was aware that despite the fact that she was very old, the *Duchesse's* eyes had a shrewd look in them as if she took in every detail of her appearance.

Arletta curtsied and waited until the *Duchesse* said:

"You are Jane Turner who has come here to teach my great-grandchildren?"

"Yes, *Madame*, I am."

"I do not believe it. You have come to the Castle to see my grandson – that is your reason for being here!"

"I assure you, *Madame*," Arletta replied, "that I am here because Lady Langley asked me to teach English to her niece and nephew, having been surprised when she stayed here recently to find that neither of them could speak their own language."

"Their own language?" the *Duchesse* retorted. "You had better not let my grandson hear you say that! He hates the English, and who shall blame him? If you are hoping to catch him, I can tell you you are going the wrong way about it!"

"You are quite mistaken, *Madame*, if that is what you think about me," Arletta protested. "I cannot imagine who has been telling you such stupid tales, which are quite untrue!"

She thought as she spoke that if Jane had been confronted with such a ridiculous assertion she would have been upset and embarrassed.

Then she remembered that poor plain Jane would never have been suspected of trying to 'catch' anyone, least of all the *Duc* de Sauterre.

The *Duchesse* looked her up and down and said:

"You are very pretty, I admit that, but this is not the right place to flaunt your looks. The sooner you go back to where you came from, the better for you and everybody else. I assure you my grandson has no time for Governesses."

"And I assure you, *Madame*," Arletta said slowly and clearly, "I am not interested in your grandson, whom I have not yet met, but only with the children whom I have come to teach."

She curtsied, turned away from the bed, and walked towards the door.

As she reached it the *Duchesse* screamed:

"*Attendez*! How dare you walk away before I have finished talking to you? Come back here immediately!"

Arletta turned round but she made no effort to return to where she had been standing. Instead she just looked at the *Duchesse*, holding her head high.

Unexpectedly the old woman chuckled.

"At least, whoever you are, you have spirit!" she said. "Most people are frightened of me."

Arletta did not speak and after a moment the old woman said:

"Come here! I want to look at you!"

Slowly, as if she was reluctant to do so, Arletta walked back to stand again beside the bed.

"You are very pretty, and you are a Lady," the *Duchesse* said in a low voice as if she was speaking to herself. "I wonder why Jacques is so anxious to be rid of you?"

64

Arletta wondered too, but there was no point in saying so.

There was silence. Then after a moment she said:

"Excuse me, *Madame*, but if I do not go now I shall be late for dinner, and I am sure that is a crime in this very punctual, well-organised household."

The *Duchesse* smiled.

"You are right about that! But I want to see you again – do you understand? I will send for you tomorrow and you can tell me all about yourself."

"Thank you, *Madame*, goodnight!"

Arletta curtsied again and walked towards the door, this time not looking back.

The footman was waiting for her outside in the passage, and he led her back by a complicated route to the foot of the staircase of the Tower.

When they reached it Arletta said: "Thank you," and the man remarked:

"Strange old lady, isn't she? People think she's a Witch! But there's a real one in the village, and if you wants your fortune told, there's no one better!"

Arletta realised he was not being impertinent, only friendly and she answered:

"I think it would be disappointing to know the future before it happens. What makes you think the woman in the village is a Witch?"

"She's one all right!" the footman replied. "You'll have to be careful not to offend her."

"I will not do that," Arletta replied, "and thank you once again."

She ran up the twisting stone staircase, thinking everything in the Castle grew stranger and stranger.

She had never met anybody quite so fantastic as the *Duc*'s grandmother.

But everybody seemed to be warning her against staying and it made her all the more determined to find out what was wrong and why they wished to be rid of her.

65

She had also not forgotten that David had said his Uncle was a murderer.

"How could it be possible?" she asked aloud, and changed into her gown, regretting she had forgotten to tell the maid to bring her a bath.

'I must make her understand that I want one every evening,' she decided.

There were enough servants for it not to be a very arduous duty with so few residents in the Castle.

At the same time there were now two more of the family than she had known of last night, and she wondered how many more lived here.

The *Comte* had dinner with them and monopolised Arletta, so that David and Pauline hardly spoke a word.

It was something which she thought should not happen, but she found it difficult to know how she could prevent the *Comte* from talking to her and paying her compliments which she found embarrassing.

She also had the feeling that they were not sincere.

When dinner was over she insisted, when he tried to inveigle her into going with him into one of the State Rooms, that she must take the children upstairs to the School-Room.

Pauline's Nurse was waiting to put her to bed, and Arletta was then alone with David.

"I can see that you do not like Cousin Jacques," he said, when the door had shut behind them.

"I have not said so," Arletta retorted.

"I told you there was something about him that is not nice," David continued.

"You know quite well I must not criticise anybody here," Arletta said.

"I will not repeat to anybody what you say to me," David said, "but you have to be careful in case somebody is listening."

"Who would want to do that?"

David shrugged his shoulders.

"The maids listen and tell Great-Grandmama, and the men spy for Uncle Etienne."

"I do not believe it!" Arletta said. "What is there to spy about?"

Again David shrugged his shoulders.

"I think you are all to isolated here," Arletta said. "I am sure you and Pauline should have friends of your own age. There must be some children in the vicinity!"

"If there are Uncle Etienne will not let us near them," David said. "But Cousin Jacques has friends."

Arletta wanted to ask who they were, but thought it would be a mistake.

When she went to bed she recalled everything that had been said and had happened, and thought it was so extra-ordinary that she really ought to write it down for Jane and send it to her in Jamaica.

"If I were clever, I could write a novel about it," she said, "although at the moment, if I am the heroine, there is certainly the lack of a hero!"

*   *   *

The following day it was a relief to learn when the *Comte* did not appear that he had gone away to stay with friends.

"It will be much nicer without him," David said darkly. "He says one thing, but his eyes say another."

"You are too fanciful," Arletta argued, although she knew he was right. "Boys of your age should be thinking of cricket, riding, shooting, and of course lessons!"

"I think of all those things," David replied, "except cricket, which Uncle Etienne says is an English game. But I am going to play it when I get to Eton, because Papa was in the First Eleven."

"My father was too," Arletta said, "and although I am only a woman, I can show you how the game is played, and perhaps we can get one of the servants to bowl for us."

David thought this was an excellent idea and Arletta went to *Monsieur* Byien.

She thought it rather strange that while she, as a Governess, was allowed to have meals in the Dining-Room, *Monsieur* Byien apparently ate alone.

She found him in his Office, and when she explained what she wanted, he looked more worried than he was already.

"I think you will have to wait and ask the *Duc* about this," he said.

"He might not come back for ages," Arletta replied. "I think it is important that David should have some idea of how this game is played, and also as he is enthusiastic, it is a mistake for him to be put off with promises."

Monsieur Byien laughed.

"Very well, *Mademoiselle*, you win! And as I played cricket as a boy, I will try first to see how rusty I am when it comes to bowling."

The gardeners made some stumps, and to Arletta's surprise *Monsieur* Byien produced a cricket bat and a ball that were ancient but serviceable.

After a little practice David began to handle his bat quite proficiently and hit the ball more times than he missed it.

It was *Monsieur* Byien who gave up first saying he was growing too old for such strenuous exercise.

But he promised to make enquiries of the younger men about the place who would practise with David the next day.

"I would rather have you," David said, "I think you are jolly sporting!"

He said this in English and Arletta laughed.

"I do not think you could have a greater compliment, *Monsieur* Byien," she said, and he had to admit that was true.

When they went back into the Castle Arletta felt she had achieved a great deal in a very short space of time, but there was undoubtedly a lot more to do.

It was a relief that evening when, after the heat of the day, Pauline was so tired that she had supper in the

School-Room with her Nurse and Arletta and David had dinner alone in the Dining-Room.

They talked in English with only occasional breaks when David wanted to say something quickly, and found his English too inadequate to keep up with his mind.

Arletta knew she had the small boy's friendship, and that he liked being with her.

She thought that today at any rate, he had forgotten to glance surreptitiously over his shoulder and say things about his uncle which horrified her.

There was no summons from the *Duchesse* and when David went to bed she thought with a feeling of satisfaction that she could rest for an hour or two before she went to sleep.

She undressed and saw that one of the pretty night-gowns which had belonged to her mother had been laid out for her on the bed, and she put it on.

Then she realised she had nothing to read.

She had meant to collect a book from the Library for herself but had forgotten to do so.

It was disappointing, she thought, then she remembered that at this time of night she had the Castle to herself.

Instead of going to her room she walked back towards the main building where the State Rooms were situated.

She knew that all the servants except for the footmen on duty in the hall would have moved into a part of the Castle that had been built very much later, in which both their bedrooms and the kitchens were situated.

"They like it there," David had explained, "because there are no ghosts in that part of the Castle."

"I have not yet seen any here!" Arletta smiled.

"I have always thought," David replied, "that ghosts only appear to people they dislike and want to frighten."

"Then if they are leaving me alone, it is a compliment I appreciate," Arletta laughed.

Now she put on the beautiful blue négligée that had

belonged to her mother, and opening her door quietly she slipped down the twisting stairs.

Her soft slippers made no sound, and anyway, there was no one to hear her.

Now as she walked through the long passages towards the State Rooms she thought it was understandable that any children, or grown-ups, living here with no other distractions would use their imaginations.

They would people the place with ghosts from the past, or turn the shadows which came from the thick fortifications of the walls into something menacing.

The sun had sunk over the horizon, but the sky was crimson and gold as Arletta entered the room that she thought was the most beautiful of all the State Rooms.

It was in the centre of the building and was known, she had been told, as the 'Ball-Room', although except for the very centre of the floor it was furnished with exquisite Louis XIV sofas and chairs and Aubusson carpets that were filled with colour.

On the walls were very old tapestries, mostly in pink. Long gilt-framed mirrors between the windows reflected them, and they seemed to blend with the colours in the sky.

It was so lovely that Arletta felt as if she was a Princess visiting the Castle two centuries earlier, and being entertained royally by the *Duc* of the day.

There was a white piano in one corner of the room inset with plaques of Sèvres china, and feeling the scene she was visualising needed music, she sat down to play a Strauss Waltz.

It seemed to blend with the room and the light from the windows, and gradually, as she played, the last rays of the sun disappeared and there was just the mystic dusk.

It was then she suddenly had an idea.

As she had entered, she had noticed in the corner of the Ball-Room a long pole with a taper on the end of it which was used to light the candles in the chandeliers hanging from the ceiling.

Then there was a little brass hood with which to extinguish them in a holder below the taper.

This was something which Arletta had seen used at home when they lit the chandeliers in the large Dining-Room when her mother had entertained.

On the piano was a small candelabrum and beside it a matchbox, and there was no reason, she thought, why anybody should know about it, if she enjoyed herself as she wished to do.

She lit the candles in the candelabrum, and then lit the taper on the pole, lifting it up to carry it to the chandelier in the centre of the room.

She could only reach the candles on the lowest tier, but she managed to light nearly a dozen of them and the whole room seemed to come to life.

She could imagine the ladies magnificent in their high wigs, wearing huge gowns with panniers on either side.

Then there were the men, also powdered and bewigged with their hair caught back in a bow at the nape of the neck, the sleeves of their elaborately embroidered coats ending with fine lace falling over their hands.

She sat down again at the piano to play music that conjured up a vision of those she could see in her mind's eye dancing a minuet in the centre of the room.

Then inevitably she came back to herself; now in the next century, she was dressed in the full skirts of a crinoline and the music for that was once again the exquisite melodies of Strauss.

Her fingers flew over the keyboard until she could not help a part of her fantasy, and she rose and stepping onto the polished floor, began to dance.

Her négligée was too narrow and she pulled it off and threw it on a chair.

Now she was attired only in her nightgown of transparently thin lawn inset with row upon row of insertions and frothing out with a wide hem of shadow lace.

There were little puff sleeves of lace, but her neck was cut low and also edged with lace.

She knew however without being told that with her fair hair and blue eyes she looked like the Princess out of a picture-book.

Now she was part of her own imagination and she swung round humming the music she had been playing beneath her breath.

She felt as if she was partnered by the tall, dark and handsome man who had always been in her dreams.

Suddenly as she swung with her arms outstretched gracefully beneath the chandelier she opened her eyes and saw him standing just inside the door of the Ball-Room.

But instead of looking at her with admiration or perhaps love, there was a look of incredulity and anger on his face.

Her feet came to a standstill and Arletta stiffened as she stared at the man who was real and not a figment of her imagination.

Then as she looked at him, there was no need for anybody to tell her that this was the *Duc*!

Chapter Four

Arletta felt as if she was frozen into immobility.

At the same time she was embarrassingly aware that her hair was falling over her shoulders, that she was wearing nothing but a nightgown, and that she was in a very humiliating position, facing her employer for the first time.

He was still looking at her as if he could not believe what he saw, and she realised that he was quite different from what she had expected.

Because everybody had said such extraordinary things about him she had imagined him to be dark and sinister, perhaps round-shouldered like the wicked Duke of Gloucester who had murdered the two little Princes in the Tower.

Instead the *Duc* was taller than the average Frenchman, and although his hair was dark he had a fresh complexion. His features were clear-cut and he was, in fact, handsome.

What, however, made him frightening, Arletta thought, was the expression in his eyes and the fact that his eyelids seemed to droop a little over them.

There were deep cynical lines from his nose to the corners of his mouth, which was set at the moment in a sharp line.

Then in a voice that seemed to vibrate on the air, he asked:

"Who are you? What is your name?"

"Arletta . . Jane Turner!"

There was a perceptible pause between the first two words because, bemused by the *Duc*'s sudden appearance, Arletta had for the moment forgotten the part she was playing and her own name came automatically to her lips.

As she spoke, she made a great effort and forced herself to pick up her négligée from the chair and put it on.

"Are you saying that you are the English Governess who has been sent here by Lady Langley?" the *Duc* asked.

"Yes . . that is right," Arletta agreed, "and . . I apologise . . but no one was . . expecting you to . . return tonight."

The words came in frightened gasps.

The *Duc* was still staring at her from under his drooping eyelids in a way she found uncomfortably intimidating, but now that she was more decently dressed and she could get her breath back, her voice sounded a little more normal as she repeated:

"I can only . . apologise, *Monsieur le Duc*. I was . . carried away by the . . beauty of the house into . . stepping back into the . . past."

"And you lit the candles on the chandeliers as well as removing some of your clothing, to create the illusion?"

The way the *Duc* spoke made it sound as if she had committed an act of indecency, if not a crime.

Arletta blushed before she faltered:

"There is . . nothing I . . can do but . . apologise, and I hope, *Duc*, you will accept my . . assurance that such a . . thing will not . . happen again."

There was silence before the *Duc* said:

"You are really the English Governess I was expecting?"

"Y.yes."

Somehow it was difficult to lie and Arletta thought even to herself that her voice sounded unsure and unsteady.

With an effort, she walked across the dance-floor and moving to the piano shut down the lid.

As she did so she was vividly conscious that the *Duc*

was watching her and once again she was aware how incompetent she must look.

"How could I have been so foolish?" she asked herself desperately.

Suddenly she was surprised to find that the *Duc* had moved and was much nearer to her than he had been a moment ago, and she asked:

"Shall I . . extinguish the . . candles?"

"A servant can do that. I think tomorrow, Miss Turner, when you are dressed more suitably for the part for which you are employed I should have a talk with you."

"Of course . . *Monsieur*."

She dropped him a small curtsy, and without looking at him again walked out of the Ball-Room into the passage.

She moved slowly and with what she hoped was some dignity until, as if she could bear it no longer, she suddenly started to run and speeding along the passages reached the staircase which led to the tower.

Only when she was in her own room did she feel as if she had encountered one of the dragons she had imagined lived in the forest, and was not certain whether she had been annihilated by it, or was actually unscathed.

'How could I have known, how could I have guessed,' she asked herself, 'that the *Duc* would return in such a strange manner?'

It was a long time before she could go to sleep.

When she awoke it was with a feeling of heaviness and apprehension in her heart in case the *Duc* thought her unsuitable and sent her back to England immediately.

There was no doubt she had astonished him, and she supposed that if he had disliked the idea of having an Englishwoman in the house in the first place his prejudice would certainly have been intensified by the scene he had found in the Ball-Room.

Therefore there was every likelihood of her being told to leave.

As she dressed she found herself praying that this would not happen.

She wanted to stay, and she knew if she was sent away now the Castle would haunt her.

It would be infuriating never to know the reason for so many things which puzzled her and for which she could find no sensible explanation.

The first thing, however, unless she was to be dismissed ignominiously, without even the opportunity of giving an explanation, was to make herself look the respectable English Governess the *Duc* was obviously expecting.

She pulled back her hair and used a dozen hairpins to hold it tightly in place, wishing as she did so that she had not left it free last night.

What would any man think of a woman who danced in such an abandoned manner, and in her night-gown?

Such behaviour on the part of a Governess was certainly indefensible.

'How could I have done anything so immodest?' she asked her reflection in the mirror.

She tried to tell herself defiantly that it was the *Duc*'s fault for surreptitiously entering his own Castle without notifying anybody of his imminent arrival.

She was quite sure that it was an unexpected visit because the servants had not talked about him, and this was confirmed when the children came from their rooms dressed and ready for breakfast to say:

"Have you heard, *Mademoiselle*, that Uncle Etienne has come home?"

"When did he arrive?" Arletta asked evasively.

"He came back after we had gone to bed," David replied.

"Now that Uncle Etienne is back he will spoil everything," Pauline answered. "He will be cross, and when he is angry, he gives me pains in my tummy."

As she put her small hand to her body, Arletta knew exactly what the child meant, and thought what she had just said might describe what she herself was feeling at this moment.

Now, wearing her most businesslike and, she thought, unattractive gown, her hair pinned back severely, she took the children down to the Breakfast-Room only to find that the *Duc* was not there.

"Where is Uncle Etienne?" David asked one of the servants waiting on them.

"*Monsieur le Duc* has had his breakfast," the servant replied.

"Good!" David remarked irrepressibly.

He sat down and began to eat heartily the hot croissants on which he spread generous helpings of the yellow butter which came from the *Duc*'s own herd of cows, and honey which came from the hives which Arletta had seen not only in the garden but almost everywhere on the estate.

She felt actually it would be better for the children to start the day with eggs or some other sensible dish, rather than with so much bread, however delicious it might be.

But she knew that to suggest such a thing would be to be told that English customs were not tolerated in the Castle, and the *Duc* would not entertain them.

She herself found that she was too apprehensive to be hungry.

Then just as the children had finished breakfast and she was going to the School-Room to start David on his English lessons, there came the summons she was expecting.

"*Monsieur le Duc* wants to see you, *M'mselle*, in the Study."

It was a command!

Feeling rather as if the tumbrels were waiting to take her to the guillotine, she walked along the corridor to the *Duc*'s Study, which she knew was near to the Library.

This was one room which she had never seen because the children had said, "That is Uncle Etienne's room!"

and hurried past as if they were afraid he might jump out at them.

There was a footman outside the door who opened it for Arletta, and she walked in, aware as she did so that the *Duc* was standing at the window, looking out onto the formal garden.

He was silhouetted against the sunlight, and she could see that, far from being bent or deformed as she had imagined him to be, he was in fact athletically slender and his clothes fitted him as if they had been made in Savile Row.

She could not help feeling he would be infuriated if he knew what she was thinking, but she had heard her father say:

"All the smartest gentlemen in France have their clothes made in Savile Row, while the smartest Englishwomen go to Paris for their gowns!"

She stood just inside the door and she thought the *Duc* was well aware that she was there.

At the same time, he deliberately delayed turning towards her, as if by doing so he asserted his authority and made her feel small and humble.

The footman shut the door behind him but still the *Duc* did not turn.

Quite suddenly Arletta ceased to feel apprehensive and afraid. Instead the pride of the Weirs, which was very much a part of their character, rose so that she felt there was no reason for her to be insulted by anybody, even if he was a *Duc*.

"You sent for me, *Monsieur*?" she said in a quiet, clear voice.

She knew as he turned round that he was surprised she should have the audacity to speak first.

She felt he looked at her deliberately up and down, as if he not only found it hard to believe what she pretended to be, but also was looking for something which would enable him to find fault.

Slowly, her back very straight, Arletta advanced a little further into the room.

Because the *Duc* had also begun to move towards her they met in the centre.

They faced each other and now Arletta made a small but graceful curtsy, and said:

"I was just about to start David's lesson, *Monsieur*, which we do immediately after breakfast until noon."

"Teaching him English!"

The way he spoke made it sound a very reprehensible activity and Arletta replied:

"That, *Monsieur*, is my reason for being here."

"I am aware of that," the *Duc* said, "but last night you certainly seemed to have made yourself very much at home in my Castle!"

There was a note of accusation in his voice that Arletta could not ignore.

"I do not think that is quite the right term, *Monsieur*," she replied. "I was not 'making myself at home' in your beautiful Ball-Room but stepping back into the past, seeing the room in the Castle as it must have been in the reign of Louis XIV."

She tried to sound brave, but there was a tremor in her voice and although she was not aware of it, her eyes were frightened.

The *Duc* walked a few paces to stand in front of the impressive marble mantelpiece.

As he turned round he said abruptly:

"You can sit down, Miss Turner."

"Thank you."

Arletta seated herself on the nearest chair, realising as she did so that its upholstery was a beautiful example of Eighteenth Century *petit point*.

She felt weak at the knees, but she had no intention of letting the *Duc* know that he was intimidating her, as she was certain any other young woman in her position would have felt.

There was silence until he said:

"Now, Miss Turner, I am waiting for an explanation as to why the history of the Castle and my ancestors should carry you away into the realms of fantasy which are unusual for a prosaic Englishwoman!"

Arletta heard the note of sarcasm in his voice that seemed to cut like the spark edge of a knife, or as if he was mentally whipping her for her behaviour.

"Even the English, *Monsieur*," she replied, "can use their imaginations. I find your Castle incredibly beautiful and at the same time very exciting."

"You are not frightened by it, or by its inhabitants?" the *Duc* asked.

"To the first part of your question, *Monsieur*, the answer is . . 'No!' To the second, I am not yet . . sure."

Arletta had the idea that at her reply the corners of the *Duc*'s hard mouth twitched a little as if he was faintly amused.

Then he said:

"Lady Langley, *Mademoiselle*, gave you a most fulsome reference, as regards both your character and your behaviour. Do you think that is consistent with the way I found you behaving last night?"

"I have already apologised, *Monsieur*," Arletta said coldly, "for I had no idea, since it was so late, that in that deserted part of the Castle I would be seen by anybody."

The *Duc* did not speak and after a moment she added:

"I came down from the Tower to get a book from the Library. I intended just to savour the atmosphere of the Ball-Room and play the piano. My dance was entirely unpremeditated – it just happened!"

"Are you given to having strange things just happen to you, Miss Turner," the *Duc* asked, "so that, as you have admitted yourself, you are swept away by your imagination? Surely a somewhat dangerous pastime for a Governess!"

The way he spoke the last three words made Arletta

certain that he was sneering at her and she replied:

"I cannot believe, *Monsieur*, that it is not in many ways a good attribute for a Governess to have imagination. After all, she needs that in order to create by her words a mental picture in her pupils."

"And that is what you do?"

"I try," Arletta replied, "and children respond because they themselves, if they are normal, always have vivid imaginations which far too often atrophy or are bullied out of them as they grow older."

She spoke positively, thinking that the *Duc* was using imagination as a weapon to make David and Pauline frightened of what they would find in England or might suffer from the English.

"I understand what you are saying, *Mademoiselle*," he remarked, "and I have a feeling that you are at the same time criticising me."

He was more perceptive than Arletta had expected and she answered:

"I would not presume, *Monsieur*, to do anything of the sort. But I am sure you are already aware that David is a very imaginative little boy, and very perceptive. Perhaps it comes from living here in this Castle; perhaps it is merely because being an orphan he has no one to whom he can turn, and has already learnt to rely on himself."

As she spoke she knew she had succeeded in surprising the *Duc*, and she added:

"Imagination for all of us can be very wonderful, and something which leads, inspires and guides us. It can also be dangerous, frightening, and in many cases restricting."

The *Duc* stared at her. Then he said:

"Again I think, Miss Turner, that you are speaking directly to me and that your words have a *double entendre*."

"If you think that, *Monsieur*, I can only apologise once again," Arletta replied. "I am concerned only with

David and with any reaction he might have to anything I teach him or to . . anything he . . hears."

She wondered as she spoke whether she had gone too far.

She suddenly had the frightening feeling that the *Duc* might consider it an impertinence and make it an excuse to be rid of her.

Instead he said:

"I find it hard to believe, Miss Turner, seeing how young you look, that you have had a great experience of teaching. And yet you talk as if you have studied Psychology for many years and concerned yourself with matters which are certainly not part of the usual curriculum."

"I am honoured, *Monsieur*, that you should think so."

There was silence and she felt the *Duc* was waiting for her to say more.

Then realising the conversation had somehow come to an abrupt end, he said:

"I feel, Miss Turner, having spoken to you, I can leave David's education in English in your hands. At the same time may I suggest that when he goes to School in your country he will need practical common sense rather than airy-fairy fantasies that cannot be substantiated."

"There I agree with you, *Monsieur*, and may I say that I feel it important for David, and Pauline for that matter, to have the companionship of children of their own age."

"Why?"

The question was sharp.

"Because, *Monsieur*, it is unnatural for children to be brought up only with grown-ups to talk to. It makes them old beyond their years, and it certainly gives rise to those fantasies of which you speak so scathingly."

She thought the *Duc*'s eyes flashed at the way she answered, but he replied, drawling the words a little as if to make them more impressive:

"French children are content to be with their families."

"Of course, I am aware of that," Arletta replied, "but

their families are usually larger than that of David and Pauline in the Castle."

As she finished speaking she wondered what the *Duc* would say, and she added:

"If you had children, David would have had a number of cousins to play with, and the same might apply to *Comte* Jacques."

As if the *Duc* had nothing more to say he remarked abruptly:

"I must not keep you any longer from David and his lessons, Miss Turner. I am only hoping he will profit by them."

Arletta rose to her feet.

"That is what I am hoping too, *Monsieur*. I am very anxious that he should look forward to going to Eton, and that he will be happy there as his father was."

She thought she saw what was an expression of scorn on the *Duc*'s face and added:

"For most boys, Eton with its games, its excellent education, and its comradeship is something that lays a foundation for them in afterlife they never forget."

She paused then said positively:

"I am convinced that David will not only find Eton very enjoyable but he will find there the companionship he needs urgently, even though he is not aware of it."

She did not wait for the *Duc* to reply but merely curtsied and walked towards the door.

As she reached it, he said:

"Inform David that he can ride with me after luncheon."

"I will tell him, *Monsieur*."

Arletta went from the room, and when she was outside and the door was shut behind her, she drew a deep breath.

After duelling with the *Duc* in words, knowing that in a way it was a confrontation between them, she felt as if it was hard to breathe.

She had expected it would be difficult to talk to him, but

the words had seemed to come to her lips as if somebody else had put them there.

Now she had the feeling she had surprised the *Duc*, and she had a great deal to think about.

'Why was I not brave enough to ask him to stop poisoning a small boy's mind not only against Eton, but against his own country?' she asked herself.

Then she comforted herself that she had not done badly for a first encounter and, what was more, as the *Duc* had not sacked her, there was likely to be another opportunity.

As she reached the School-Room David gave a cry of delight and jumped up from the table of soldiers at which he had been sitting.

"You are all right?" he asked. "Uncle Etienne was not disagreeable to you?"

"No, I am all right," Arletta replied. "And now let us get on with your lesson. You should have written the essay I set you yesterday instead of playing with your soldiers."

"I was too worried in case Uncle Etienne sent you away."

"Why should you think he would do that?"

"Because you are English, and because when he came back last night you were playing the piano in the Ball-Room."

"How do you know that?" Arletta gasped.

"I heard Uncle Etienne's valet, who came back with him, telling one of the servants that as they walked up to his bedroom they heard music, and Uncle Etienne went to see where it came from. Were you not frightened being in that part of the Castle in the middle of the night?"

"It was not quite the middle of the night, for you had only just gone to bed," Arletta replied. "As I told you before, David, I am not frightened of ghosts, which I think are just tales to frighten the foolish, and as I did not know your Uncle was returning, I did not expect anybody to hear me playing."

"If you had asked me, I would have come with you."

"That is very sweet of you," Arletta replied, "but I was just thinking how beautiful the Ball-Room was and I wanted to hear the music of a Strauss Waltz being played in it."

She tried to make light of what had happened, being certain that as soon as she was discovered the story had run through the Castle like wildfire.

"I think you are very brave," David said, "and I am quite certain none of the other servants would have dared to go to the Ball-Room alone."

He paused, then he said eagerly:

"How did you light the candles on the chandelier?"

Arletta told herself she was right. The story of her behaviour was being gossiped about from the *Duchesse* down to the lowest scullier.

"I will tell you all about it later," she said firmly. "Now we have to do our lessons."

"Uncle Etienne did not tell you we were to stop them?"

"No, of course not," Arletta answered. "He knew I was coming here to teach you, and I think, David, you are making your uncle into a monster, a dragon or an ogre, whichever you like – just because you have nothing else to talk about."

"People talk about him because they are frightened of him," David said, "and everybody says that he killed his wife!"

"If that is true he would have been guillotined!" Arletta answered sharply.

"Somebody pushed her over the battlements," David said in a low voice, "and there was no one else there except Uncle Etienne. Everybody says they hated each other and quarrelled all the time!"

Arletta slapped her hand down on the table.

"I am not going to listen to all this gossip," she said. "It is horrid, it is wrong for you, and quite frankly I do not believe a word of it!"

David shrugged his shoulders.

"You may not believe it," he said, "but everybody in the Castle does, and when the *Comtesse* died just when she was expecting to marry Uncle Etienne, everybody said he killed her because he no longer wanted her to be his wife."

Arletta sighed.

"If you are going to go on talking such nonsense, David, and saying such wicked things, which I am sure are lies, I am just going to talk French to you, and refuse to teach you any more English."

"That is unfair," David objected.

"It is you who are being unfair," Arletta retorted. "In England a man is innocent until he is proven guilty. It may be different in France, but all I can say is that in any civilised country, if your uncle had done the wicked things of which you are accusing him, he would have been brought before a Judge and Jury, and hanged or guillotined."

"He got away with it because he was so clever!" David replied.

"If he did . . good luck to him!" Arletta said. "Personally, I think the whole thing is a lot of rubbish thought up by a lot of gossiping women who have nothing better to think about!"

She spoke angrily because she thought it was so bad for the small boy to think such terrible things about one of his relations, and to relate them almost with glee.

Then feeling she was perhaps taking the wrong tack she said:

"Listen to me, David. This must have all happened a long time ago, and I think because you are very intelligent you ought to refuse to believe what people are saying about your Uncle unless they can prove to you positively without any question of doubt that he is a murderer!"

David was intrigued, as she had expected he would be.

"How could they do that?"

"I do not know," Arletta answered, "but as I have said, in England a man is innocent until he is proved guilty. When in future people say things about your uncle like that I suggest you say: 'Prove it, prove it, then I will believe you!' That is the only just and right way for a gentleman to behave and it is also the sporting way."

"You are right," David said after a moment. "Perhaps it is a mistake to believe that it was Uncle Etienne who pushed Aunt Theresa over the battlements. Nobody knows if she cried out for help, or if she threw herself over."

"Now that is a very sensible attitude," Arletta approved.

"The *Comtesse*," David went on, "who was very beautiful, died of poison, through taking too much laudanum. They say that Uncle Etienne gave it to her in her coffee."

"She might have put it in herself," Arletta suggested.

"They say she did not want to die, they say she wanted to marry him."

"They say! They say!" Arletta repeated. "They say anything to make a good story! Again, David, you are not to believe such wicked things unless you can actually prove them. Find somebody who actually saw your uncle putting the laudanum into the coffee, or who can prove that he bought it especially to do a thing so wicked!"

"I see what you mean," David said slowly after a moment. "A man would not buy laudanum, would he?"

"Laudanum is a drug that some silly women take because they cannot sleep," Arletta replied. "But I never heard of a man taking it, unless he was wounded and a doctor gave it to him. When my Father was in terrible pain the Doctor said he could have some, but he waved him away and said it was only women who made themselves insensible."

As she spoke, Arletta remembered that she had often wished her father was not so brave and would allow himself to be doped.   At least it would have given her a little respite from his fault-finding, his swearing and his continual complaining.

She thought David was puzzling over what she had said and after a moment she suggested:

"Now, shall we forget your uncle and things that happened years ago, and try to get on with the future? Every minute that we waste talking about your uncle is a minute off your efficiency when you yourself go to Eton."

David sat himself down at the table and pulled the book towards him.

"Shall I go on translating what we were reading yesterday?" he asked.

"I am listening," Arletta smiled.

When they went to luncheon, she was glad to see that *Comte* Jacques was there, because she thought it would divert the *Duc*'s attention from herself and the children.

She was right in that *Comte* Jacques immediately began to talk to the *Duc* about the estate, his horses, and later the political situation in Paris.

But she was well aware that while he did so he kept looking at her, and she felt anxious in case the *Duc* might notice it.

She could imagine nothing more uncomfortable than that he should think she had been encouraging the *Comte* to pay her compliments.

She had not forgotten that the *Duchesse* had said how *Comte* Jacques wished to be rid of her.

Rather than annoy the *Duc* unnecessarily she spoke to the children in French, at the same time saying as little as possible, so as not to appear to be pushing herself forward.

'If I say nothing I expect he will think I am dull,' she thought, and decided that a Governess's position was a very precarious one, in which it was not possible to please everybody, least of all one's employer.

* * *

When luncheon, which had been a delicious meal, was ended, the *Duc* and David went riding together.

There was a little pang in her heart as Arletta watched them go, wondering if her riding had come to an end.

Perhaps the *Duc* would forbid her to ride or else himself always accompany David, which would mean there was no reason for her also to be mounted on one of his magnificent horses.

At the same time she was acutely conscious of him sitting like a King at the end of the table.

He was magnificent but he also had such a strong personality that she felt she had to look at him and listen to him.

'I hate him!' she told herself; but she knew it was not true.

She was intrigued and fascinated by the strangest and most amazing man she had ever encountered.

Having seen them off, she started to walk rather disconsolately back to the School-Room, and in a way was not surprised when she got there to find the *Comte* waiting for her.

Pauline, she knew, was with her Nurse, and would lie down for an hour before they went into the garden.

There was a smile on the *Comte*'s lips as she entered the room that made Arletta wary.

"I hope, *Monsieur*," she said, "you do not need me, for I have some very important letters to write."

"Of course I need you," the *Comte* replied, "and I missed seeing you yesterday, as I hope you missed me."

"I was far too busy," Arletta answered.

"You cannot pretend that the chatter of two children is enough to satisfy somebody as intelligent as you are. Besides I have a lot to say to you."

"I can only reply that is unfortunate," Arletta said, "as I have some letters that must catch the evening post."

"Very well, I will not keep you long," the *Comte* agreed, "so come and sit down, Miss Turner, as what I have to say is very important."

Reluctantly and with the feeling there was nothing else

she could do without seeming rude. Arletta sat down on a chair and the *Comte* sat opposite her.

Then as if he felt they were too far away from each other, he rose to take a chair next to hers, and saying as he did so:

"You are very lovely! I cannot understand why you should waste your looks and your brain on anything so mundane and boring as teaching children."

"Actually, I do not find it boring," Arletta replied, "but extremely interesting. My problems are not with the children, but with the grown-ups."

If she had thought to embarrass him she was mistaken, for he threw back his head and laughed.

"You are very frank, Miss Turner, but that of course is a typically English trait. Although I know that no Englishwoman can accept a compliment gracefully, let me tell you that you are very beautiful and very desirable."

"If that is all you have to say to me, *Monsieur*," Arletta said, "I am going up to my bedroom to write my letters."

She would have risen from the chair, but the *Comte* said hastily:

"What I have to say is important. I want you to consider very, very carefully the proposition I am making to you."

"Proposition?" Arletta repeated.

"It is that you should let me take you to Paris to show you the gaieties, the amusements of what to me is the most attractive City in the world."

Arletta looked at him. Then the expression in the *Comte*'s eyes answered the question on her lips.

"I cannot believe, *Monsieur*," she said quietly, "that you intend to insult me!"

"Do you really think it is an insult that I should want to make you happy, give you beautiful gowns and a great deal of jewellery, none of which will shine as brightly as your eyes?"

90

"You are insulting me!"

She rose to her feet as she spoke and the *Comte* rose too.

"Can you be so foolish as not to understand that if you accept my offer you will be a sensation in Paris? Every man to whom I introduce you will be at your feet!"

"And what will that mean?" Arletta asked.

"Fame, success, riches, a position for which most women would give the eyes out of their heads!"

"In which case, *Monsieur*, I suggest you offer it to them! As far as I am concerned, never in any circumstances, even if I were starving, would I agree to degrade myself by accepting such a proposition!"

"Then let me make it more attractive," the *Comte* said, "by telling you how much you excite me, how much I want you, and how very happy I could make you."

He drew closer to her as he spoke, but Arletta stepped back.

"Unfortunately, *Monsieur*, you do not attract me!" she said. "Therefore, strange though it may seem to you, I would rather be a Governess than your mistress!"

The *Comte* stretched out his arms but she evaded him by slipping round the back of the chair.

Swiftly she moved to the door before he could reach her, and as she left the room she looked back to say:

"The answer *Monsieur*, is firmly, definitely, and decisively – 'No!' "

She did not wait for his reply, but pulled the door sharply to and hurried up the twisting stairs to her Bedroom.

After locking the door in case he should follow her, she recalled exactly what he had said and thought that it was not only an insult, but there was an ulterior motive behind his suggestion.

David had said there was something insincere about the *Comte* that did not ring true, and Arletta would have been prepared to swear that she did not really attract him as much as he pretended.

In which case, why was he offering to spend so much money on her?

It was a puzzle which made her stand at the window staring out for a long time at the fields and open country stretching away to the great woods.

Just below the window out of which she was looking was the river.

She stared down at it, thinking that in the past it had been a natural barrier against enemies who tried to storm the Castle.

'Now the enemies are within,' she thought.

She wondered if the *Duc* had any idea how strangely his relatives behaved or what was said about him, according to David, by everybody.

It was very frightening, Arletta thought, but there was more to it than that.

She could think now more clearly of how he had looked at luncheon sitting at the top of the table in his heraldic chair.

He had seemed a Royal figure who ruled over his domain with a hand of iron, and fought his enemies in battles in which Arletta was certain he always returned the victor.

Now his adversaries were using a 'whispering campaign', which was far more difficult to combat.

'Can he really have murdered two women?' Arletta asked herself.

Her instinct told her the accusation was untrue, though she had nothing positive to go on.

It was obvious that the *Duc* inspired fear and that he was a dominating figure with a personality that made other people feel small and uncomfortable.

Human nature being what it was, that inevitably made them dislike him.

But murder was a very different thing, and thinking of him – the way he looked, the way he talked and moved – Arletta could not imagine him conspiring to kill, then covering up his crime with an air of innocence.

It was something that seemed alien to such a man, although why she should think so, she had no idea.

'There must be some other explanation,' she thought, and wished she could talk to somebody other than David about it.

On an impulse, because she felt perturbed and upset not only by the *Duc* but also by the *Comte*'s suggestion, she thought she would visit the Church she had seen on her arrival just outside the gates of the Castle.

She put on a shady hat because the sun was hot and went down the stairs cautiously, hoping that by this time the *Comte* would have left the School-Room.

The door was open and there was no one there.

With a sigh of relief Arletta went on down the passage which brought her to a side-door where there were no footmen in attendance.

She saw no one and let herself out into the courtyard.

Walking quickly in case she was noticed by the *Comte*, she passed through the huge gates and out into the small village outside them.

The Church was less than fifty yards away, and when she entered it she realised how old it was and how beautiful.

The rounded pillars rose up to an arched ceiling and the walls were enormously thick, while the nave was so small that the congregation was obviously quite limited.

Yet because it was so old there was an air of sanctity and faith that Arletta recognised.

She knelt down at the end of the Church and looked at the altar.

It was very quiet, and because the windows were small and the glass in them very old there was little light except in the Sanctuary, where a few flickering candles had been lit in front of a statue.

Arletta found herself praying that she would be able to help the children and perhaps, although it seemed an extraordinary request, move the shadow of fear from the Castle itself.

"It is so beautiful, God," she said, "and beauty should mean love, not hatred."

When she rose from her knees she had a sudden wish to light a candle, knowing that Catholics believed that as long as the candle was burning, the prayers they had said would soar upward to Heaven.

She felt in the pocket of her gown and found to her surprise that there was a small coin there.

It was in fact a shilling that she had intended to put on the offertory plate on the last Sunday she went to Church, but for some reason she had taken the money instead from her handbag forgetting what she had in her pocket.

She was sure the priest would find a way of changing English coinage.

She put it now in the small iron box and taking a candle from where they lay at the foot of a statue, she lit it.

"Please listen to my prayer," she said as she did so.

She looked up to find the saint to whom she was praying was Joan of Arc.

She gave a little smile to herself thinking how inappropriate it was when the *Duc* condemned the English for burning her at the stake.

Arletta thought now that wherever she might be, the Saint would be working for friendship between the English and the French to prevent there being any more wars between them.

St Joan's voices would tell her they must learn to love each other even though they were so different in so many ways.

'*Grandmère* would understand that,' Arletta thought.

For the first time since she had come to the Castle she prayed to her French grandmother to help her to understand and help her countrymen.

"They are partly mine too, *Grandmère*," Arletta said and felt almost as if she could see her grandmother's white hair and beautiful face, smiling at her as if in approval.

Having genuflected to the altar, she left the Church and went out into the sunshine.

As she did so she saw coming from the Castle gates, dressed in his ordinary clothes since he was off-duty, the footman who had escorted her to the *Duchesse*'s room.

"You're here, *M'mselle*!" he exclaimed in surprise.

"Yes, I am here, Jean!" Arletta replied.

"I see you've been to Church," Jean said. "And now you're in the village, you must come with me to see the Witch."

"Oh, no, I cannot do that!" Arletta said quickly.

"Why not?" he asked. "No other village has a Witch as clever as seeing into the future as ours! Come on, I'll take you to her. I've known her all my life. I'm sure she'll be curious about you."

"I . . I do not think . . ." Arletta began.

Suddenly she thought it would be very interesting.

She had never met a Witch before, and although she knew Witchcraft and Witches had always played a part in French History she had never imagined she would have the chance of speaking to one.

Quite suddenly her hesitation seemed rather foolish and she said:

"All right, Jean, I will come with you, but you will have to lend me some money to give her, for I have nothing with me."

"That's all right," Jean said. "I'll pay for you and you can pay me back when you get your wages."

"I will pay you back before that," Arletta said. "I do not like to be in debt."

Jean laughed.

"Proud are you, *M'mselle*? I'd always heard you English give yourself airs!"

He was teasing her and Arletta merely smiled.

She knew that he was not being impertinent, but

friendly, and she thought in some unaccountable way he, like the Castle, was different from what she had expected.

'I might as well be prepared to accept everything,' she told herself, 'even Witches!'

Chapter Five

The cottage to which Jean took her was very small with a low doorway, under which he had to bend his head.

Inside it seemed dark until as Arletta's eyes adjusted themselves she saw, sitting in front of the fire although it was a warm day, a very old woman.

She was wrapped in a dark shawl and her thin hair, which was grey streaked with white, was pinned back at the nape of her withered old neck.

She had strong features with a hooked nose which made Arletta think that perhaps it was the way she looked more than anything else that had made her a Witch.

"I've brought a client, Granny," Jean said, and the old woman looked up.

"Who is it?" she asked.

Arletta drew nearer and saw that the Witch had cataracts over both her eyes, which must have made her completely blind.

"I am new to the village," she said quietly, "and Jean thought I should meet you as the most important inhabitant."

The Witch chuckled.

"Is that what he said? Well, some people find me important, and some are frightened of me."

"I am not frightened."

Jean opened the old Witch's hand and put a silver coin in it, saying as he did so:

"You tell the Lady about herself, Granny. I expect as she's very pretty, you'll find something exciting for her in the future."

Having spoken he grinned at Arletta and went out of

the cottage shutting the door behind him.

There seemed when he had gone a strange silence, almost, Arletta thought, as if the old woman in front of her had moved away into another world.

Arletta sat down opposite her and did not speak, and after a few moments the Witch said:

"You're from overseas, and you're hiding something about yourself!"

Nervously Arletta looked back just to be certain Jean was not listening to what was being said.

The door was, however, fast shut, and the Witch went on:

"I see you puzzling – worrying – afraid. There's danger, real danger! I see blood!"

Arletta drew in her breath.

Still she did not speak, and after a moment the old Witch went on:

"Beware, be ready, and protect yourself. When the trouble that will happen comes, you must rely on yourself. Remember that I told you so."

Her voice seemed to die away, and as she apparently had no more to say Arletta said gently:

"I will remember what you have told me, but it sounds rather a dismal picture."

"Some people are winners," the Witch said after a moment, "and you are one."

"Thank you," Arletta replied, "but I am not certain what race I want to win."

The old woman chuckled.

"The race of life, my dear, and we're all competing in that!"

"You really think I am a winner?"

"You will win!" the Witch said.

Then, as if she wanted Arletta to be sure she had finished, she lay back in her chair and shut her eyes.

Arletta looked at her for a moment, longing to know more, wondering if she dared ask about the *Duc*, but knew that was impossible.

Then she said once again:

"Thank you!" and rose to her feet.

The old Witch did not reply and she went out of the cottage to find Jean leaning against a tree, waiting for her.

"Was she good?" he asked. "What did she tell you?"

"It was rather gloomy," Arletta answered. "She said there would be trouble, but she did say I was a winner."

"I'm sure that's true," he said, "and you've cheered us all up, *M'mselle*, in the Castle, just because we can look at you."

Arletta gave a little laugh, but she did not reply.

She thought it was a mistake to be too familiar about herself to Jean, who she was quite certain was a *Don Juan* in the village.

She therefore held out her hand saying:

"Thank you very much, Jean, for being so kind to me. I will give you back the money which you lent me the next time you come to the School-Room."

"That's all right," Jean replied.

He realised that Arletta did not wish him to accompany her any further, and he therefore touched his cap and walked away down the narrow street, while Arletta went back to the Castle.

She had just walked into the main hall and was going up the stairs when *Comte* Jacques appeared.

"Miss Turner!" he called. "I want to speak to you!"

"I am going to the School-Room."

"Very well," he said, "I will come with you."

There was nothing she could do to stop him and they walked in silence along the corridor which led to the tower.

When they entered the School-Room Arletta hoped that Pauline would be there, having finished her rest.

But the room was empty.

She took off her hat and started to tidy some books which had been strewn on the table in the middle of the room.

The *Comte* shut the door and stood looking at her before he said:

"Have you considered the suggestion I put to you earlier?"

"I gave you my answer at the time," Arletta replied coldly, "and it is still 'No!' "

"Women invariably change their minds!"

"That may be true of some women, but I have no intention of changing mine. Quite frankly, *Monsieur*, as I consider what you said to me insulting, I do not wish you to refer to it again."

"Can you really be so foolish?" he asked. "You know that you would enjoy Paris and all the amusing things I can show you, apart from the fact that I will teach you about love."

There was a note in his voice which Arletta knew was dangerous and she said quickly:

"It is time for me to give Pauline her lesson in English, so if you have nothing sensible to say, *Monsieur*, I must ask you to leave."

The *Comte* laughed softly and came towards her.

He moved swiftly and had his arms around her before she could realise what had happened.

She gave a cry of protest, then struggled against him. As he drew her closer in spite of her efforts, she realised how strong he was and that he intended to kiss her.

"I want you!" he said. "Whatever you feel about me is of little consequence because I want you!"

Now there was a note in his voice which told her that he was not pretending, that she genuinely excited him, and there was a fire in his eyes that was unmistakable.

"Let me go!" she cried pushing him away from her with both her hands on his chest, knowing how ineffectual she was being as his lips were almost touching hers.

She turned her head frantically first one way then the other to try to avoid him.

She felt his mouth warm and insistent against her cheek.

100

Then as she gave another cry, knowing she was completely helpless, the door opened and as the *Comte* released her, Pauline came running in.

"I'se late, *M'mselle*," she cried, "but I fell asleep and *ma Bonne* did not wake me!"

Breathless, and feeling her heart beating in an agitated manner, Arletta managed to answer:

"You are not too . . late . . for your lesson . . and as it is such a . . lovely afternoon . . we will go into the garden."

She realised her voice was coming in jerks as she spoke, but Pauline did not seem to notice.

Instead she was looking at the *Comte* and said:

"I do not want you, Cousin Jacques, to listen to my lessons. You laugh when I make mistakes."

"I do not laugh at *Mademoiselle* Turner," he replied.

His eyes were on Arletta and she knew that instead of being angry he was amused by what had happened.

He was confident she would eventually capitulate and do what he asked of her.

Because she felt she could not bear to be near him for another moment she picked up her hat from where she had put it on a chair and said to Pauline:

"Come along, let us go into the garden just as we are, and you can tell me the names of the flowers and the birds in English."

"I can remember some of them, *Mademoiselle*."

Pauline slipped her hand into Arletta's as she spoke and without either of them giving another glance at the *Comte* they went out of the School-Room and down the stairs towards the door which led into the garden.

In the sunshine as she began to teach Pauline, Arletta felt her agitation subside.

At the same time she was aware that if this was the danger of which the Witch had spoken, it was something that would happen again and again.

She wondered how she could possibly persuade the

Comte to leave her alone, and even for one moment contemplated speaking to the *Duc*.

Then she was sure that as he hated her for being English, he would be certain it was her fault and that she had encouraged the *Comte* to behave so insultingly.

'What can I do, what can I do?' she asked herself.

It was a question that was at the back of her mind all the afternoon as they wandered round the beautiful gardens.

They sat at length on a stone seat beneath a statue of Aphrodite.

Looking back at the Castle silhouetted against a cloudless blue sky, Arletta felt it was so lovely that it was wrong for so many conflicting and unpleasant emotions to be harboured in it.

How could anybody living amid such beauty have nothing but hatred in their hearts?

She must have been silent for some minutes because Pauline became bored and jumped up from her side to run away towards the fountain.

Arletta knew she was watching the goldfish swimming in and out of the water-lily leaves in the stone bowl.

She thought as she looked at the child with the water rising up behind her that this was another picture which as far as she was concerned would be unforgettable.

Then to her astonishment a voice said beside her:

"What are you thinking about, Miss Turner?"

She looked up to see that it was the *Duc*.

He had obviously just come back from riding, for he was wearing his riding-breeches and jacket.

She would have risen, but he said: "No, do not get up," and sat down beside her.

"If you are back, *Monsieur*," she said, "I should go to find David."

"David wanted to practise over the smaller jumps in what I call my Riding-School," the *Duc* replied. "I have left my Head Groom with him, so he does not require your attention."

As he spoke in his usual dry, rather cynical manner, he made Arletta feel as if she was being needlessly fussy.

She turned her head away to look again at Pauline by the fountain.

"I would be interested to know, Miss Turner, what you think of my Castle," the *Duc* said.

Arletta smiled.

"I was thinking just a minute ago, *Monsieur*, that it is so beautiful that everybody who looks at it and lives in it should think only of love and not of anything wrong or evil."

"Love is something with which most women are mainly concerned," the *Duc* said cynically.

"I do not mean that kind of love!" Arletta said sharply. "I mean the love of beauty which one finds in the country-side, in your garden, and which should be present in a building that is so old and so perfectly preserved."

"I stand corrected!"

Arletta knew he was being sarcastic and she said:

"Perhaps you think it very impertinent of me, *Monsieur*, but while you are entitled to be cynical if you wish, it is wrong for children and, quite frankly, I am worried in case, being orphans, David and Pauline should grow up with the wrong ideas about life."

She felt as she spoke that she was being extremely brave to tell the *Duc* the truth.

But she told herself that perhaps it would make him think that he should not show his feelings so obviously.

The *Duc* looked at her before he said:

"I have a feeling, Miss Turner, that even for an Eng-lishwoman you are a very unusual type of Governess."

"I think all Governesses are concerned with their charges and it is not just a question of teaching lessons, but also teaching them about life."

"And that is something about which you know a great deal?" the *Duc* remarked, and once again he was being sarcastic.

"I suppose the truth is," Arletta replied, "that I know very little, and that is why I still, *Monsieur*, have illusions and ideals; and I have no wish to lose them here."

She knew as she spoke she had surprised him and he said:

"You have made your point, Miss Turner! I shall certainly think over what you have said to me."

He rose abruptly from the stone seat and as he walked away Arletta wondered if she had offended him. Perhaps she had made a mistake.

She thought it was time they returned to the Castle and the School-Room, and she therefore called Pauline. They went back through the formal garden, the little girl telling her about the goldfish as they went.

They went through the garden door, and as they reached the passage which led up to the School-Room she saw the *Comte* waiting for them.

As she had no wish to speak to him, Pauline ran ahead up the steps to the tower.

When Arletta would have followed her the *Comte* seized her waist and stopped her.

"What was my cousin saying to you?" he demanded fiercely.

Arletta, who had been expecting him to ask something very different, looked at him in surprise.

"Does it matter?"

"I want to know!"

There was something fierce about the way the *Comte* spoke and the expression in his eyes.

"It was not very interesting," Arletta said quickly. "He was just explaining that David had not returned to the School-Room but was practising over the jumps."

"Is that all?" the *Comte* enquired.

"That is all of any consequence."

As she spoke Arletta twisted her wrist free of his hand and walked away.

She had the feeling that he was watching her until she

disappeared through the School-Room door.

She could not believe he was jealous, and yet at the same time there was something sharp about his questions that told her he was perturbed because the *Duc* had spoken to her in the garden.

'He is certainly very tiresome,' she told herself.

Then she wondered once again how she could persuade him to leave her alone.

* * *

That evening, to Arletta's surprise, there were several guests for dinner.

Among them were the *Marquis* and *Marquise* de Vasson, who lived, Arletta learnt, about six miles from the Castle.

The *Marquise* de Vasson was an extremely beautiful woman who was just at the age when her youth was a little behind her, and middle-age just a few years ahead.

She sat on the *Duc*'s right, and because Arletta found it fascinating to watch the French visitors she was quite certain before dinner ended that the *Duc* and the *Marquise* had at one time been very close to each other.

It was obvious that she was still attracted to him and used every wile to hold his interest, and perhaps to try to revive the flame that had burnt itself out.

Arletta had no idea why she should know these things.

Yet although she had expected a Frenchwoman to be flirtatious when she was with an attractive man, she knew instinctively with a perception she was not aware she possessed that the *Marquise* was still infatuated with the *Duc*.

He spoke to her in his dry, cynical manner, and there was nothing in his expression or in his half-closed eyes to make Arletta think that his feelings were in any way unusual.

And yet she knew, almost as if somebody had told her so, that at one time he had felt very differently.

The *Marquis* was a much older man with white hair, slightly deaf, who talked incessantly and extremely boringly on subjects which were not particularly interesting to anybody else at the table.

The *Comte* also had near him two middle-aged but good-looking women, who were very anxious to entertain him.

Arletta knew that he was bored and was aware that his eyes kept straying down the table to where she was sitting with the children.

That was also true of another man in the party, the husband of one of the women beside the *Comte*.

Arletta was certain he was the local Roué, the type of elderly man who would pursue any young girl, if he had the chance.

He had singled her out before dinner when the children had been taken to the Salon to meet the *Duc*'s guests.

She noted that David bowed in the French fashion over the ladies' hands, and Pauline dropped little curtsies to everybody.

Arletta stood in the background, remebering how her own Governess had behaved when she was a child, but to her surprise the *Duc* had her brought forward and introduced her, saying:

"I know you will be astonished to know that I have an Englishwoman in the Castle, but David and Pauline's Aunt, Lady Langley, who was here recently, insisted they should learn English, which is, as you are well aware, something I have no intention of teaching them myself!"

There was laughter at this and the *Marquise* put her hand on his arm and said in a voice that was full of meaning:

"Why should you, my dear *Duc*, teach anything but the Art in which you are supreme and unchallenged?"

"You flatter me!" the *Duc* said dryly, and continued to introduce Arletta to his guests.

She had not made the mistake of dressing up when she heard there was to be a dinner party.

Instead she had worn the most severe evening gown she

possessed, which actually was very becoming, and had deliberately arranged her hair in a manner which she thought most appropriate to a Governess.

However, because it waved naturally, no matter how tightly she dragged it back, in a few minutes it was in waves against her oval forehead, and because her hair was so long it was impossible to wear it in a bun, so it was arranged in a chignon at the back of her head.

'Nobody will notice me,' she told herself, 'and all I have to do is to look neat and tidy.'

But as Jane had thought, Arletta made everything she wore seem a perfect frame for her figure, and there was nothing she could do to alter her large eyes which dominated her small, pointed face.

"And are you a very strict Governess?" the old Roué asked her in a low voice.

"I try to be," Arletta replied.

"I think, *Mademoiselle*," he said, "your lips were not made for speaking English to the *Duc*'s nephew and niece, but for kisses!"

To Arletta's annoyance she found herself blushing before she turned away to speak to Pauline.

She was well aware during dinner that the Roué was watching her from the other side of the table.

In fact, wherever she looked she encountered either his eyes or the *Comte*'s.

When dinner came to an end she was relieved to be able to take Pauline upstairs, although David stayed with the guests a little longer.

Then just as Arletta was thinking she would go to bed the boy came into the School-Room, and when he saw her he smiled and said:

"They talked about you when you had left, *Mademoiselle*."

"What did they say?" Arletta enquired.

"They all said you were too young and too pretty to be a Governess! The *Marquise* told Uncle Etienne she would find somebody better than you to teach us."

"And what did your uncle reply to that?" Arletta enquired.

"I spoke first," David said, "and I told the *Marquise* you were a very good Governess and I had learnt a lot of English, and I had no wish to have anybody else!"

Arletta was touched.

"That was very sweet of you, David."

"They all laughed at me," David said a little resentfully, "and the fat man with the red face said: 'You are quite right, my boy, you keep her while you have the chance!' "

"Thank you," Arletta said. "And now as it is late you had better go to bed, otherwise we shall waste time in the morning, and that would be a mistake."

"My English is better, is it not, *Mademoiselle*?" David asked anxiously.

"You have worked very hard and I am very proud of you," Arletta answered. "I do not believe anybody could have learnt English faster than you have, but there is still a lot to do."

"I know that," David replied, "and before I go to sleep I talk to myself in English, and I try to think in it too!"

"That is very, very sensible of you."

For the first time since she had been in the Castle she bent her head and kissed him.

To her surprise he put his arms around her and gave her a hug.

"I like being with you, *Mademoiselle*," he said.

She had the feeling he was missing his mother, and hugged him back before she answered:

"Goodnight, David, sleep well, and happy dreams!"

"I should say that to you," David said, "in case the ghosts come to haunt you."

"I doubt if they will do that," Arletta smiled, and went upstairs to her Bedroom.

The maid had left a small oil lamp burning by her bed which was turned low, and she crossed the room to turn it up before she went back to the door to lock it.

It was then, to her surprise, she found that the key which had been there the night before and every night since she had come to the Castle was no longer there.

She thought it must have fallen out and looked on the floor, but there was no sign of it.

Then suddenly she was nervous.

Suppose the *Comte*, after what he had said, came to her room?

She could hardly believe he would do such a thing, and yet the way he had spoken when he tried to kiss her had been frightening.

Then she remembered the manner in which he had questioned her about the *Duc*, and she thought he must be jealous.

If he came late at night there would be no one to hear her if she screamed, except for the children, and she was certain they slept soundly.

Arletta suddenly felt very young and helpless, and knew that Jane had been right when she had warned her against Frenchmen.

It seemed inconceivable that the *Comte* could behave in such a dishonourable way to a woman who was employed by his cousin.

Yet she had the inescapable feeling that the explanation of her key having vanished was that he had taken it.

'What shall I do? What shall I do?' she asked herself.

She felt she must ask somebody to help her, but she knew that really the only person to whom she could appeal was the *Duc*, and that was impossible.

She thought of going to find the Housekeeper and asking if she could change her room, but then she remembered how everybody gossiped in the Castle.

If she said anything about a missing key it would make the staff suspicious.

Speculation as to who had taken it would run from room to room like wildfire and would certainly reach the *Duchesse*'s ears.

'What shall I do?' she asked again.

She thought the *Comte* was far more frightening than any ghost could be.

Suddenly she had an idea.

The first day when David had taken her round the Castle he had shown her the Armoury.

She had seen the cannon, the bows and arrows, and the old muskets that had been used by the private Army of the *Ducs* of Sauterre.

But also in the huge room, which was at the bottom of one of the towers, there had been a cabinet in which was displayed a number of smaller weapons.

"Some of these," David explained, "were given as presents to various *Ducs* by Kings, Princes, Sultans and Sheiks."

Because the small boy had been in a hurry to show Arletta everything in the Armoury, she had only time for a perfunctory glance at the cabinet and what it contained.

Now she remembered she had seen a small revolver set with jewels.

"What is that?" she had asked, attracted by the glittering stones.

David did not answer. He had moved away, but she saw written on a card the date it had been presented to the then *Duc* by the Tzar of Russia.

Because she was sure it was the only thing that might help her now, she ran as quickly as she could down the twisting staircase of the tower.

Arletta found her way with some difficulty to the Armoury.

It was on the other side of the Castle, and while some of the rooms were lit by gas, the oldest part had either oil lamps or candles.

When she came to the end of a long passage where the candles were in sconces, there was only darkness, and she realised she would have to carry one with her.

It was the only light to guide her the rest of the way to the Armoury.

110

To her relief the door was not locked and she walked in, feeling the cold from the unplastered walls, and aware that it was what the children would have called 'creepy' because the ceiling was so high and everything was dark and still.

She remembered where the cabinet was situated and walked across the stone floor to it.

It was not locked. She raised the lid and looked down at the miscellaneous collection of swords, daggers and duelling pistols.

It was quite easy to see what she was looking for because the amethysts with which the handle of the revolver was studded and the small diamonds surrounding them flashed in the candlelight.

Arletta put down the candle and lifted the revolver.

She had often fired not only her father's shotgun but his revolver, which was not very up-to-date.

He had also been amused when she had tried firing the duelling pistols which had belonged to her great-grandfather. He was reputed to have been such a dashing Buck that he had fought innumerable duels when George IV was Prince of Wales.

The revolver might be elaborately decorated but it appeared to Arletta to be quite a serviceable weapon.

She also saw to her relief that there was a little pile of bullets which had been dipped in gold lying beside it.

She picked them all up and carrying them and the revolver in one hand and the candle in the other started back on the somewhat tortuous journey to the tower occupied by her and the children.

When she reached the lighted part of the long corridor she put the candle back in the sconce from which she had taken it.

Suddenly as she walked on she heard voices and stopped. Someone was coming; quickly she hid herself in the shadows of a large doorway.

She then realised that what she had heard were the

voices of some of the guests. They were moving from the Salon into which they had gone after dinner, and she wondered why.

Then as they drew nearer, she realised two people were approaching her down the passage and knew they were the *Duc* and the *Marquise*.

She pressed herself even further into the darkness of the doorway in which she had hidden, and then, afraid that she might be seen, she swiftly turned the handle of the door behind her and slipped into the room.

She left the door slightly ajar and through the crack she saw the *Duc* and the *Marquise* pass down the corridor, her arm linked in his.

"I have missed you, Etienne," Arletta heard the *Marquise* say. "How can you make me live without seeing you? It is cruel, unbelievably cruel!"

"People were talking about us, Justine," the *Duc* replied, "and you know that is a mistake from your point of view."

"It may be a mistake, but I love you," the *Marquise* replied, and Arletta heard the pain in her voice.

They moved on and she could no longer hear what they said. She guessed they were going to look at the small Aviary which was a little further along the passage, and which she had passed earlier without realising it.

There were quite a number of small unusual birds in it, and Pauline loved them.

Arletta supposed the *Marquise* had made her desire to see the Aviary as an excuse to take the *Duc* away from his other guests.

For some reason she could not understand, she felt it painful to know the *Duc* was listening to the lovely woman on his arm.

When she knew they were no longer in the corridor she sped as quickly as she could to her Bedroom without seeing anybody else.

She put the revolver down on the dressing-table and

knew, now that she had the protection of it, that she was no longer helpless.

It seemed to her that when she held it in her hands she could think more clearly, and there was no reason to be in a panic.

As she loaded the revolver she realised that the bullets were so small that they could not kill a man unless he was struck in a very vulnerable place.

But it would certainly be extremely painful if a bullet pierced someone's arm or leg.

'Now I feel safe,' she told herself, and putting the gun down she started to move the furniture in the room in front of the door.

Arletta found a chair that was high enough to insert under the handle, but which alone, she was aware, might be pushed aside if any great force was exerted against it.

Then she moved a chest of drawers with some difficulty, because it was heavy, against the rest of the door.

'That will certainly keep out the *Comte*!' she thought with satisfaction.

In the meantime, having undressed and got into bed, she put the small revolver under her pillow, feeling quite proud of herself for being so self-sufficient.

"The Witch was right," she said aloud, "I shall win this battle."

Then she remembered with a little feeling of horror that the old woman had seen blood.

'Once he knows I have a revolver,' she reasoned to herself, 'he will not be such a fool as to risk my shooting him.'

It was a frightening thought, but because she was very tired, and it had been a hot day, she fell asleep.

* * *

When Arletta awoke, it was to find that the sun was coming through the curtains of the windows, and it was morning.

She sat up in bed, and looking across at the furniture

she had piled in front of the door, she wondered if the *Comte* had tried to come to her, as she had feared he might do.

She had the feeling that he had done so, but on finding the door barred had not risked making a noise by trying to force it open.

She could not be sure; she only knew that she had slept without being disturbed, and that was more important than anything else.

She put back the furniture before the maid came to call her.

When she was dressed she went downstairs with the children to the Breakfast-Room.

She wondered if when she saw the *Comte* she would be able to tell if he had come to her Bedroom or not.

To her surprise however, there was no sign of him or the *Duc* and the servants explained that the *Comte* had left early to spend the day with friends, and the *Duc* as usual had gone riding.

The morning passed in a quiet, normal fashion, with David having his lessons until, to Arletta's joy, they went riding.

She thought as she rode one of the most magnificent horses she had ever known that she was so happy that it was worth any difficulties, even those occasioned by the *Comte*, to be at the Castle and have so many privileges.

They had ridden through the Park and Arletta was just thinking it was time they returned home for luncheon when she saw a magnificent figure on a horse coming towards them, and she knew it was the *Duc*.

"Oh, here comes Uncle Etienne!" David said in a disagreeable tone of voice. "We do not want him finding fault with us!"

"Perhaps he will praise us," Arletta suggested. "You know, David, he has been very kind and good-tempered about your having an English Governess."

"That is true," David agreed. "I thought he would make far more fuss about it."

"Be nice to him," Arletta said quickly as the *Duc* reached them.

"Good morning, Uncle Etienne!" David said as the *Duc* raised his hat to Arletta. "Can I show you how fast I can go now on *Le Roi*? It is the biggest horse I have ever ridden!"

"I shall be interested to see your progress," the *Duc* replied.

David rode towards the long flat piece of land where the *Duc* had just been riding.

Then he touched his horse with his whip and set off at a tremendous speed.

The *Duc* watched him with a faint smile before he said to Arletta:

"I suppose we had better follow him, Miss Turner. Have you enjoyed your ride?"

"This is the most wonderful horse I could ever imagine!" Arletta replied.

"By that I assume you ride in your dreams."

"Only when I can be on a horse as marvellous as this."

She thought he was amused by her reply but he did not speak as they were now riding a little more quickly towards the end of the field where David was waiting for them.

As they trotted side by side the *Duc* remarked.

"I see you have been well taught!"

"My father was very insistent that I should ride correctly."

"I am sure he was not disappointed in you."

It was almost a compliment, and Arletta looked at him with laughter in her eyes as she said:

"I was thinking just before you joined us that to have horses like this to ride would make up for all the other disappointments and problems in life."

"Have you many problems?" the *Duc* enquired.

Arletta, remembering the *Comte*, looked away from him.

115

"A few."

"Perhaps I could solve them for you."

Arletta was so surprised at the suggestion that she stared at him in astonishment. Then she said quickly:

"No, no! Of course not! I have to learn to look after myself, and that is what the Witch told me I must do."

"The Witch?" the *Duc* questioned. "Do you mean to tell me you have been to see that old charlatan?"

He spoke angrily and Arletta thought she had been indiscreet.

But by that time they had reached David, and there was no need for her to say anything more.

"That was good, was is not, Uncle Etienne?" the small boy asked.

"Very good!" the *Duc* said. "I know if your mother had been here, she would have been very proud of you."

Then without saying any more he rode off and left them.

For a moment Arletta and David just sat on their horses watching him go.

Then David said:

"Did you hear what he said, *Mademoiselle*? He praised me, and that is something he has never done before!"

Chapter Six

At luncheon there was only the *Duc* and it was a great relief to Arletta that the *Comte* was not there.

To her surprise the *Duc* seemed in a very good temper and told interesting stories about the Castle, and she thought that for the moment, at any rate, he had ceased hating her.

He was pleasant too to the children, and did not sneer at them or speak disparagingly about their learning English.

"What are you going to do this afternoon?" he asked as luncheon finished.

There was a little pause before Arletta replied:

"I had hoped, *Monsieur*, that David and I might go riding again as it is such a lovely day, but of course if you think it is too much, we could do something else."

"I think it is an excellent idea, if you keep under the trees where it is cool," the *Duc* said, "and as I do not think you have visited one of the more interesting of my woods, I will show you the way."

Arletta was surprised by the offer but accepted gratefully. He led her and David in a different direction from the one they had taken before, and they entered a wood where the trees were much more mature.

She found it fascinating, especially as the *Duc* pointed out the different birds they saw.

He also seemed to be in such a good temper that David chattered away to him without any sign of the fear and dislike he had shown previously.

In the very centre of the wood was a very old Chapel which had been built almost at the same time as the original Castle.

It was never used, the *Duc* said, but when they dismounted and went inside Arletta felt as if the same sanctity she had felt in the Church was there.

All the furnishing had been taken away, leaving only the bare stones of its walls. Birds had nested in the rafters, and there were lizards running over the walls.

Yet she thought that for the animals of the forest, at any rate, it was still a place where they could find sanctuary from hunters or predators.

She did not say so aloud, but as if the *Duc* could read her thoughts he said:

"I used to think when I was a boy that the animals that were wounded by sportsmen or perhaps by some other animal came here and the spirits of the monks who once officiated looked after them. Now you are thinking the same thing."

"How did you know what I was thinking?" Arletta questioned.

He smiled enigmatically and said:

"Your eyes are very revealing, *Mademoiselle*!"

She felt shy and when they rode on again she left David to talk to his uncle while she first listened and then joined in the conversation.

At the same time she was sure, with a feeling of relief, that the *Duc*'s hatred for her as an Englishwoman was not so intense as it had been when she first arrived.

She hoped now that for the children's sake there would be a happier atmosphere at the Castle than she had sensed at first.

'He has such a strong personality,' she thought, 'he must use it to inspire people around him.'

And as she heard the *Duc*'s deep voice answering one of David's questions, she added:

'He should be a leader . . .'

There was a little pause and a voice inside her mind she could not control added: 'with love.'

When they returned and entered the hall, a footman

informed Arletta that the *Duchesse* wished to see her.

She had known for the last two days that the *Duchesse* had been unwell and had not wanted to see anybody.

When she had changed her riding-habit for one of her simple gowns, a footman escorted her to the *Duchesse*'s apartments.

She was looking even more fantastic, Arletta thought, wearing a ruby necklace round her throat, huge rubies in her ears, and the same stones round her wrists and on her fingers.

As Arletta neared the bed the *Duchesse* looked at her with the shrewd searching expression in her eyes that she had noticed before.

"Come and tell me what you are up to, young woman!" she said. "I hear that Jacques is pursuing you and that you have been riding with my grandson."

Because Arletta could not help it she gave a little laugh.

"Why are you laughing?" the *Duchesse* asked.

"Because, *Madame*," Arletta replied, "you know everything that happens in the Castle, even though you are confined to your Bedroom."

"What else have I got to interest me, except the vagaries and peculiarities of other people?" the *Duchesse* asked.

Arletta did not answer and the *Duchesse* went on:

"What has Jacques been saying to you? I am told he is pursuing you, but it is unusual for him to interest himself in Governesses. Are you encouraging him?"

"I assure you, *Madame*," Arletta said coldly, "that I have told *Comte* Jacques quite positively to leave me alone, and I only hope he does so."

"Setting your sights a little higher?" the *Duchesse* enquired.

"I am setting my sights on making certain that David speaks perfect English by the time he goes to Eton," Arletta replied. "He has made tremendous progress as he is very anxious to learn, and therefore it is coming easily to him."

"So you think you are a very efficient teacher, do you?" the *Duchesse* asked.

"I hope so," Arletta replied.

The *Duchesse* looked at her as if she was trying to penetrate deeper, below what appeared on the surface.

Then she said:

"Tell me more about yourself, *Mademoiselle*, I am extremely curious!"

"You would find me a very dull subject, *Madame*," Arletta answered, "and if you will excuse me, I want to be with Pauline, who will be feeling very neglected, as I have been so busy with David all day."

"Any excuse to get away, I suppose," the *Duchesse* said almost to herself. "Never mind, nothing can be hidden forever, and sooner or later the truth will out!"

"So I have always been told, *Madame*," Arletta said, "but if one is not afraid of the truth, why should one worry?"

She curtsied to the old woman, and then without waiting for her to say any more, walked across the room.

She half-expected by the time she reached the door to be called back, but the *Duchesse* did not speak and with a sense of relief Arletta found herself outside in the corridor.

The old maid was waiting for her and she said almost apologetically:

"You mustn't mind anything *Madame la Duchesse* says to you, *M'mselle*, even though it may seem rude. She's very old and is ill most of the time but still dislikes being left out of everything."

"I can understand that," Arletta said gently.

"She's worried too," the maid went on, "about the things *Comte* Jacques tells her about the *Duc*."

Arletta guessed what these were and she said:

"Perhaps you could persuade *Madame* that *Comte*

Jacques is not always to be relied upon. If you ask me, I think he is a trouble-maker!"

She thought as she spoke that she was being indiscreet.

But she was quite certain *Comte* Jacques was telling the *Duchesse* stories about the *Duc* and herself and trying to whitewash his own behaviour, which she thought disgraceful.

"I wish he would go away," she murmured to herself as she walked back to the tower. "The place is much happier without him!"

She gave Pauline a short lesson from the books they had brought from the Library while David translated into English two pages of a history book.

When they had finished he said:

"There is still one place in the Castle which you have not yet visited, *Mademoiselle*, and that is the dungeons."

"After all the horrid things I have heard about them, I am not interested," Arletta answered.

"Why not come with me now?" David suggested. "I am surprised you have not heard the groans and cries of the prisoners."

"Do you mean the dungeons are under this tower?" Arletta asked.

"Most of them," David said. "There is one which has a trapdoor which swings down to leave a huge hole in the floor."

"I have heard about those sort of traps," Arletta said, "and I think they are very cruel!"

"One *Duc* de Sauterre in the Seventeenth Century had a crueller trap than anybody else," David said, as if it was something to be proud about. "When he pulled the lever the victim fell through a trapdoor into a cage which was embedded deep in the bottom of the river where he drowned."

Arletta thought this was against all the rules of war whereby there was always the chance that prisoners could be exchanged or released when the war was over.

The idea of dungeons and traps made her shudder and she said:

"Do not let us talk about it, David, and quite frankly I do not wish to see your dungeon."

"They are a long way beneath us," David said cheerily, "so there is no reason to think about them unless you hear the ghosts of those who died groaning, as the servants think they do."

"I have not heard or seen any ghosts since I have been here," Arletta said firmly, "and I am now convinced that all the talk about them is just foolish superstition."

She then suggested the children should go to the Aviary to feed the birds, and as they were delighted to do so they hurried off down the passage where she had seen the *Duc* and the *Marquise* the previous evening.

Although she told herself it was none of her business she could not help thinking of the two of them together, and the way the *Marquise* had said to the *Duc* that she loved him.

As the children ran from cage to cage giving the birds the seeds and the fruit they enjoyed, she wondered if, when the *Duc* made love to a woman, he looked as bored and cynical as he did at other times.

Then she told herself it was very immodest for her to think about such things.

Yet, because in his own way he was so outstanding and different from any other man she had ever seen before, it was impossible not to think about him.

"I would like to have a little bird of my own," Pauline said, "I could have it in a cage in the School-Room, and listen to it singing."

"You will have to ask your uncle if you can have one, but I can see no reason why not."

"I am sure Uncle Etienne will say 'no'," Pauline complained.

"There is no harm in trying," Arletta replied.

"He was very nice to me today," David said.

"Who was nice to you?" a voice asked from the doorway.

Arletta looked round and felt her heart sink.

Comte Jacques had come into the Aviary when she had hoped they would be free of him for a time.

As if he felt he had to answer David said:

"I was talking about Uncle Etienne."

"Why was he nice to you?" the *Comte* enquired.

"*Mademoiselle* and I went riding with him. He took us to the old Chapel in the wood, and it was very interesting!"

David spoke almost defiantly as if he expected the *Comte* to say it had been nothing of the sort.

Instead the *Comte* looked at Arletta in what she thought was a strange manner before he said:

"So my estimable cousin has been pleasant, has he, despite the fact that you are English?"

It was what Arletta had thought herself, but there was no need for *Comte* Jacques to emphasise it.

It was something he would doubtless talk about to the *Duchesse* in such a way that she would put a very different construction upon it.

"I think," she said in a cold, repressive voice, "that *Monsieur* has accepted that it is essential for David to speak English properly before he goes to an English School."

"And of course he is very fortunate in having such an attractive, charming and intelligent teacher."

Arletta sighed to herself.

She found it very tiresome that the *Comte* went on paying her compliments, and was, she was sure, still expecting to persuade her to accept his invitation to Paris.

He, of course, had no idea how insulting it was to her not being the Governess he thought her to be.

It was something he would never have thought of suggesting if he had known her real identity, and he would not have dared to put such a 'proposition', as he called it,

123

to a French girl with a protective family behind her.

"I think it is time we went back to the School-Room," Arletta said to the children.

"All right," David agreed.

Pauline was taken reluctantly away from the birds, still saying she wanted to have one of her own.

The *Comte* did not speak as Arletta, holding Pauline by the hand, went from the Aviary.

Yet she knew he was watching her, and she could feel his eyes almost as if they were boring their way through her white skin.

'He is tiresome, and I have no wish to have anything to do with him,' she told herself.

At the same time, she remembered the revolver she had locked away in a drawer in her Bedroom and knew how glad she was to have it.

There was no one else for dinner except the *Comte* and once again the *Duc* was pleasant and, Arletta thought, extremely interesting.

She found herself discussing with him the pictures in the Castle and realised he was surprised she knew so much about Art.

It was with great difficulty she refrained from telling him that in Weir House there was a collection of family portraits that was noted as being one of the finest in the whole of England.

As the *Duc* had so much to say, the *Comte* was surprisingly quiet, and when Arletta took Pauline away upstairs she thought, although she was not sure, that he looked at her resentfully because she had ignored him.

There was certainly an expression in his dark eyes that she did not like.

She knew that once again she would pile the furniture in front of her door, and sleep with the little Russian revolver under her pillow.

However, because it had been an active day, she did not lie awake worrying about the *Comte* or anybody else, but fell asleep soon after she had got into bed.

She was dreaming that she was riding a very large horse when suddenly she came back to consciousness, aware that something had disturbed her.

Her thoughts immediately went to the *Comte* and she lay in the darkness listening, wondering if what she had heard was an attempt by the *Comte* to open the door.

She wondered whether in the morning she should ask the Housekeeper for another key or suggest that a bolt be fixed which would prove just as effective.

Then she was quite certain that if she said a word about the missing key to any of the servants, it would be a story that would be repeated and repeated over the whole Castle.

She knew exactly what the *Duchesse* would say, and she told herself she could not bear to think of how it would be whispered amongst the staff and how they would look at her speculatively as if it was her fault that the key had gone.

'I will manage as I did last night,' she thought.

Actually it had needed a considerable amount of strength to drag the chest of drawers again in front of the door, but it was certainly preferable to knowing that everybody was talking about her.

Now for some seconds there was no sound, and thinking she must have been mistaken she turned her head sideways on her pillow ready to go back to sleep again.

Then suddenly she heard a cry that was quite different from the sound she had expected, and although it was not very loud it was a sound like a shriek of pain.

It flashed through her mind that this came from the ghosts about which David had talked so much, and was what she had been told to expect to hear ever since she had first slept upstairs in the tower.

Just for a moment a sense of fear seemed to invade her whole body, and as the shriek came again she shut her eyes as if she was afraid an apparition would appear in front of her in the darkness.

Then as she trembled, and was ashamed of the fact, her common sense told her that whatever the servants might say, ghosts do not as a rule make a noise.

Now the shriek was repeated and as she listened Arletta was almost certain it came from some small animal.

The cry grew worse and more persistent and she told herself it must be a rabbit or a cat which had been caught in a trap.

It was impossible to ignore it so she sat up in bed and lit the oil lamp which she had blown out when she was ready to sleep.

She realised the sound came from the West window in her room which looked out over the fields towards the woods.

Because the cries were continuing and seemed to Arletta to be getting even more agonising, she got out of bed and opened the window as wide as possible.

She leaned over the sill which was the thickness of the tower walls to look out.

The river was directly beneath her on this side of the tower and she knew there were some trees and shrubs on the other side of it before the open fields.

Now she realised the sound came from directly below her, in fact at the foot of the tower, and although it was impossible to see she was sure some animal was caught in a trap.

'Perhaps I could release it,' she thought.

She knew the only way to do so would be to go to the bottom of the tower where the dungeons were situated.

'It would be better to wait until morning when it is light,' she thought.

Then she knew as the shrieks continued that it would be impossible for her to sleep knowing that some creature was suffering so intensely.

She wondered if it would be possible to find one of the

servants and tell them what was happening.

But she had the feeling they would not be particularly interested as long as it was not a human being who was crying out in such agony.

'I must be sensible and forget it,' she decided.

But she knew it was impossible to sleep or to rest and know that some little creature was suffering.

Resolutely she first lit the candles on her dressing table, then put on the blue satin négligée which the maid had laid over a chair.

As she buttoned it down the front, Arletta realised that it had a pretty lace-trimmed pocket on one side of it.

She thought that if she could see the animal in the trap from one of the windows it would be kinder to shoot it than let it suffer.

Her father had always said that when a hare, a fox, or even a dog had been caught in a gin-trap, which was a particularly cruel type, there was no chance of saving their leg which would have been broken, and the flesh lacerated, and the quicker they died the better.

Arletta hated the idea of killing anything, but she knew it was far more kind than to let the animal continue to screech in agony.

She therefore put her hand under the pillow and drew out the little Russian revolver and slipped it into the pocket of her négligée.

As she pulled the furniture away from the door she knew that if she carried one of the candles the draughts that blew through parts of the Castle might cause it to be blown out, so she picked up the oil lamp.

She went slowly down the twisting stairs, lighting her way with the lamp, and when she reached the corridor it was easy to see her way by the candles in the silver sconces.

There was nobody about and having reached the ground floor she continued down a narrow staircase which she knew, although she had not been there before, led to the dungeons.

She had only taken a few steps when a voice behind her asked:

"What are you doing? Where are you going?"

She was startled so that the oil in the lamp swung a little precariously before she turned round.

It was the *Duc* who stood above her at the entrance to the stairway and because for the moment she could not speak, he asked again:

"What are you doing at this time of night, and why are you going down to the dungeons?"

He was still wearing the evening clothes he had worn at dinner and Arletta was immediately conscious that she was wearing a négligée and her fair hair was falling over her shoulders, as he had seen it once before.

As she looked up at the *Duc* she saw the expression on his face was not exactly one of anger, but, she thought, of suspicion.

It flashed through her mind that he thought she was meeting somebody surreptitiously, perhaps the *Comte*, in the dungeons.

Quickly, because she was embarrassed she answered:

"There is an animal caught in a trap, *Monsieur*, and it is screaming in pain. It woke me up."

"An animal?" the *Duc* repeated.

"Yes, *Monsieur*, it is directly below my window in the tower."

"And you say you cannot sleep?"

"I was asleep, but I knew I could not ignore it when it was in such agony."

Arletta felt she was explaining herself badly and thought for a moment he did not believe her.

Then he said:

"If that is so, we must certainly do something about it. Let me take the lamp from you."

He came down the stairs which were wider than those at the side of the tower.

He took the lamp from her hand then went ahead,

holding it high so that it lit the way.

Down, down they went, and as Arletta followed the *Duc* below ground, she thought he must think her very foolish.

When the stairs came to an end and they were in a circular chamber on the same dimensions as the tower above it, she was aware that opening out of it were heavy iron doors that she knew must be the entrance to the dungeons.

It was then, almost to her relief, that she heard faintly the screams that had awakened her and she knew the *Duc* must hear them too.

He was, in fact, standing in the centre of the chamber waiting for her to follow him down the last few steps.

He turned his head towards the sound of which Arletta had spoken and said:

"It obviously comes from here."

He opened the door of one of the dungeons, and now the noise as it echoed round the stone walls seemed almost deafening.

The dungeon was very small and was barely high enough for a man to stand upright, and there was a window just below the stone ceiling which was heavily barred with only an inch between each of the bars.

Arletta knew that even in the daytime the window was too small to let in very much light, but this was where the sound was coming from.

Holding the lamp as high as he could the *Duc* moved to the window and as Arletta followed him she saw that tied to one of the iron bars was an animal struggling to free itself, and screaming as it did so.

For a moment it was just something dark which made it difficult to determine what it could be.

Then as the *Duc* shone the light on it she saw it was a small cat with black and white fur.

It was little more than a kitten but old enough to make an almost deafening noise, and the *Duc* looked at it for a long moment before he said:

"Hold the lamp for me while I release it."

"It will fall into the river," Arletta said quickly.

"I think it will save itself, if it is freed," he replied.

She took the lamp from him and he struggled to undo the knot of the cord which fastened the cat's leg to the iron bar.

Because it would have been impossible to have squeezed the cat through the bars, Arletta knew two people must have been involved in torturing the wretched animal in such a hideous manner.

She could not see the *Duc*'s face because he had his back to her, but she knew perceptively that he was very angry.

'It must have been somebody in the Castle who has done this,' she thought.

She wondered if the *Duc* would find out who the culprit was and what punishment he would inflict upon him.

It seemed to take a long time before he finally pulled the string into the dungeon, and as he did so the cat gave a shrill scream as it fell down into the river or against the foundation stones of the Castle.

But whichever it was, after it had vanished there was silence and the *Duc* turned towards Arletta.

She saw he was frowning and she asked:

"Who could have done anything so cruel?"

"That is what I would like to know," the *Duc* said ominously.

"I will tell you who it was," a voice said from the doorway.

They both turned round and as they did so the *Duc* took the lamp from Arletta as if he wanted to see who had spoken.

To her astonishment it was *Comte* Jacques.

"You know who tortured this wretched animal?" the *Duc* asked harshly.

"I did!" the *Comte* said. "It was a 'sprat to catch a mackerel'. But what a surprise! My bait, a very effective one, has captured not one fish, but two!"

"I do not know what you are talking about," the *Duc* said, "but you can tell me when we get out of here."

"That is where you are mistaken, my dear Cousin," the *Comte* replied. "You are not leaving here, not for a moment or two. I think you will understand what I mean when I tell you I have my hand on the lever of the trapdoor."

The *Duc* stiffened and Arletta felt as if her heart had suddenly stopped beating.

She saw now that, exactly as David had described it, just inside the dungeon there was a lever and the *Comte*'s right hand was resting on it, as he himself was standing in the round chamber at the door of the dungeon.

He had only to exert a little pressure and the floor would open beneath them and they would fall down into the cage at the bottom of the river where they would drown.

It all flashed through her mind.

At the same time she thought she must be dreaming, and what was happening could not be true.

"What are you talking about, Jacques?" the *Duc* asked.

Now he was speaking quietly and deliberately slowly, slightly drawling his words.

"I think you understand my dear Cousin, or at least you should by now," the *Comte* replied, "that I have no intention of allowing you to be involved with a young woman, however attractive, however fascinating."

"I have no idea what you are saying to me," the *Duc* said, "and I suggest we leave this very unpleasant, cold, damp place and talk sensibly outside."

"I enticed *Mademoiselle* here," *Comte* Jacques said, "because when I saw you looking at her in a way I considered dangerous to my future, I knew if she disappeared without any trace, as I planned, who would be blamed!"

"Of course," the *Duc* agreed, "there would be no doubt about that!"

The *Comte* laughed, and Arletta thought there was a mad note in his merriment.

"No one had any idea, did they, Cousin Etienne," he jeered, "that it was I who pushed your wife over the battlements! You left her crying, and it was easy, almost too easy, to make sure she did not produce the son who would have disinherited me."

As he spoke Arletta started, and she began to understand now what this was about.

"As you say," the *Duc* said slowly, "you were very clever, and no one suspected you, Jacques."

"I made sure of that," he boasted.

"I suppose," the *Duc* said, and now his voice was as cynical as it had been when Arletta first arrived at the Castle, "you also killed Madeleine Monsarrat!"

"Of course!" the *Comte* replied. "It was easy, because she was always drinking coffee, to put an overdose of laudanum into her cup. Poor Cousin Etienne, you really have been very unjustly accused."

"I am only surprised that you have left me alone for so long!" the *Duc* remarked.

"I was just a little worried in case your sudden disappearance might focus on the fact that I am the next *Duc*," the *Comte* said. "But now you and the delectable English teacher will disappear and of course I shall spread the rumour that you have run away together. There will be no other possible explanation."

Arletta gave a cry.

"How can you think of . . anything so diabolical . . so wicked?"

As if for the first time she drew his attention, the *Comte* said.

"You have no one to blame but yourself! I tried to take you away from the *Duc* if you remember, by inviting you to come with me to Paris."

"I cannot really believe you ever thought I would consider such an idea!" Arletta said angrily.

"Why not?" the *Comte* asked. "We would have enjoyed ourselves together, I would have made sure of that, and I should not have been afraid of my cousin becoming infatuated with you, as he was with the *Comtesse*."

"But you . . cannot . . mean to do anything so . . terrible as to . . kill us!"

Arletta tried to speak pleadingly, but her voice trembled and she knew how frightened she was.

"I am told that drowning is quite a pleasant death," the *Comte* answered, "and although I shall be sorry to lose the company of my delightful and charming cousin, I shall make up for his loss by being a most exemplary and dashing *Duc!*"

He looked down at Arletta as he spoke and she knew it was only a question of seconds before he pulled the lever.

"Now listen, Jacques," the *Duc* said harshly, "I have something to suggest to you."

"What is it?"

"Drown me, if you wish to," the *Duc* said, "but spare *Mademoiselle*'s life. She has nothing to do with our quarrels or the succession of the *Duc*s de Sauterre. She is English. Let her go back to her own country and forget she has ever been involved in anything so unsavoury."

The *Comte* laughed, and it was a very unpleasant sound.

"An heroic suggestion!" he sneered, "but I am not quite so foolish, my dear Cousin, as to let a woman free who would talk – and what woman would not talk in such circumstances?"

He laughed again and said:

"There is nothing you can do – nothing! I have beaten you, as I always wanted to, and I have won!"

As he spoke the word 'won' it brought back to Arletta the Witch's words that she was a winner, and also that she was the only person who could save herself.

She thrust her right hand into the pocket of her négligée

and grasped the butt of the little jewelled revolver.

"Good-bye, Cousin Etienne!" the *Comte* was saying triumphantly, "I am sorry there is no time for you to say your prayers!"

Before he could finish the last word Arletta drew out the revolver and shot him.

The explosion seemed to echo deafeningly around the small chamber, and she felt almost as if it cracked her ear-drums.

Then as the *Comte* took his hand from the lever to put it to his shoulder where the bullet had struck him, the *Duc* stepped forward.

Regardless of the fact that he held the oil lamp in his left hand, he hit the *Comte* with the clenched fist of his right hand on the point of the chin.

With a groan he staggered back against the stone wall, then slid slowly down from it to the floor, unconscious.

As he did so his evening coat flew open and Arletta saw the crimson blood already staining his white shirt.

The *Duc* turned back to hold out his hand to Arletta.

As she clutched it, feeling as if it was a lifeline, he pulled her out of the dungeon into the chamber outside.

It was then that the horror of what had happened swept over her and she held onto the *Duc*, hiding her face against his shoulder.

He put the oil lamp down on the protruding part of a buttress and put both his arms around her.

"It is all right," he said gently, "Is is all right, and you have saved us both."

"D. did I . . k.kill him?"

It was difficult to speak the words because her teeth were chattering.

"No, he is alive," the *Duc* replied, "but I will deal with him later."

Still with one arm round her he drew her back to the door through which they had entered the chamber and shut and bolted it, leaving the *Comte* inside.

Then he said:

"I have to carry the lamp. Do you think you can walk up the stairs?"

"I am . . all . . right."

The *Duc* did not take his arm from her, but picking up the lamp to light their way, they moved slowly side-by-side up the stairs, until they reached the corridor at the top.

There was a table in the passage just beside the entrance to the stairway and the *Duc* put the lamp down on it.

Then, aware that Arletta was almost fainting, he picked her up in his arms.

She wanted to protest that she could manage to walk, but the words would not come and instead she hid her face against his shoulder, and as she did so, she started to weep.

As the *Duc* carried her back along the passage and up a few stairs, she did not look or even wonder where they were going.

She merely went on crying against him.

Only when he stopped walking and put her feet down on the ground, still keeping his arms around her, did she raise her head.

"It is all right, *ma Chérie*," he said very quietly. "we are both alive and, I promise you, this will never happen again."

The way he spoke, the deepness in his voice, and the endearment seemed to seep through the sense of shock that Arletta was feeling and check her tears.

She raised her face, looking up at him in bewilderment, and as she did so, his arms tightened and he drew her closer.

He did not speak, but she she had the strange feeling that she could feel her heart beating against his.

Then his lips came down on hers.

Chapter Seven

For a moment all Arletta could feel was the hardness of his lips against hers.

Then as he held her closer still and felt her mouth soft and trembling, his kiss became more insistent, more demanding.

Because she had never before been kissed, Arletta had no idea that it would mean sensations rising within her that were different from anything she had known or imagined.

And yet it was all the rapture of her dreams, all the beauty of her imagination enveloping everything she saw and felt.

The *Duc* kissed her until she felt as if she had died and in some amazing manner was in Heaven.

It seemed impossible that she could be alive and on earth, and feel at the same time that she was part of the music of the spheres with angels singing around her.

When she thought it was impossible to feel any more, while her body quivered with the rapture that was so inexpressible and so wonderful that she could only pray that it would never stop, the *Duc* raised his head.

He looked down at her, at her eyes wet with tears, and yet shining with a radiance that seemed to light the School-Room into which he had carried her.

For a moment they just looked at each other, but when he would have kissed her again Arletta gave an inarticulate little murmur and hid her face against his neck.

He held her close against him, his lips on her hair, then said in a voice that sounded deep and unsteady:

"You must go to bed; my precious, and I must deal with

that devil below who intended us to die."

"How . . could he have . . done such . . terrible things to . . you?" Arletta whispered.

Her words, because of the depth of her feeling, were almost inarticulate, but the *Duc* heard and said:

"You are thinking of me?"

"I . . I had to . . save you."

"As you did, most effectively."

He was aware as she was speaking to him that she swayed, and he picked her up in his arms and carried her from the School-Room onto the twisting staircase.

There was just room for him to take her up past the rooms where the children slept and into her own Bedroom.

Although she had taken with her when she went to the dungeons the oil lamp that was beside her bed, she had left two candles alight on either side of the mirror on her dressing-table.

The *Duc* carried her to the bed and laid her down very gently.

As he looked down at her she put her hands up to him and said with a touch of fear returning to her voice:

"P.please . . do not . . leave me."

"I must," he answered, "but you will be all right."

"Will you . . come back and . . tell me if the *Comte* is dead?" Arletta faltered.

Then with a little cry she added:

"If he . . d.dies . . will I have to . . stand trial?"

The *Duc* sat down on the bed and took her hands in his.

"There will be no trial!" he said. "Jacques is not dead, which in some ways is a pity. At the same time, I will deal with him and try to put right all the evil he has done."

There was a hard note in his voice as he spoke and Arletta held onto him as she said:

"You are . . quite certain if you . . go back to him now that . . he will not . . manage in some way to . . k.kill you?"

"You would mind if he did?" the *Duc* asked.

She looked at him for a moment, not understanding what he was saying.

Then as she realised, the colour crept up her face, and the *Duc* thought it was the most beautiful thing he had ever seen.

"There is no need to answer that, *ma Belle*," he said. "You love me as I love you, and we will talk about it later."

He bent forward and she thought he would kiss her lips, but instead he kissed her forehead.

"Get into bed and rest," he said. "I may be sometime, but I promise I will come back to tell you what has happened."

He kissed her head and then as she watched him, her eyes seeming to fill the whole of her face, he went from the Bedroom closing the door behind him.

She listened until she could no longer hear his footsteps going down the stairs.

Then she shut her eyes as if she could not believe that she was not dreaming the strange and terrible things that had happened.

At the same time what she remembered more vividly than anything else was the feel of the *Duc*'s lips on hers.

* * *

A long time later, as the first faint glow of the dawn was breaking in the sky, the *Duc* knocked gently on the door, then came into Arletta's room.

She was lying back against the pillows, her long fair hair falling over her shoulders.

She had been unable to sleep and instead was praying, praying fervently, that now that the *Comte* had been unmasked and his wicked plotting against the *Duc* exposed there would no longer be the whispering in the Castle that there had been before.

She understood now why it had affected everybody who was living there, including the children.

It had poisoned the atmosphere and prevented it from being, as she wanted, a Castle of happiness and love.

'Now the *Duc* can be happy and look happy,' she told herself.

Then, as if a knife pierced her heart, she thought there would be no reason, now that she had saved him, why he would want her after she had finished teaching David English.

There would be women as beautiful as the *Marquise* who would love him even though they were married.

There would be other women like the *Comtesse* the *Comte* had killed, whom he would love and who would make him a suitable wife without running any danger of being exterminated.

'He kissed me just in gratitude,' she told herself.

While to her it had been the most wonderful thing that had ever happened, to him she was just another woman he had kissed in a long line of them.

'I love . . him,' she admitted at last, and knew it was inevitable when he was so handsome, so magnificent.

At the same time, because he had been cynical and unhappy, it had in a way been a challenge that she could not resist.

She thought she had wanted to help him, or at least find out about him, perhaps from the first moment she had seen him, staring at her in astonishment as she had danced under the chandeliers in the Ball-Room.

Looking back, she had first been intrigued by what Jane had told her about him, then by the way the *Duchesse* had accused her of trying to 'catch' him, and of course, by all the things everybody in the Castle and the children had told her.

'Now the darkness and shadows that spoiled everything have been lifted,' she thought. 'I have saved his life, and there is nothing more I can do for him.'

She tried to think about it logically and calmly, yet she could only remember his arms around her and the way his lips sent thrills through her whole body.

She felt again the ecstasy he had given her and the rapture that was part of her prayers. She knew it was not only something she could never forget, but which she would never find with any other man.

It was a white and worried little face that Arletta turned towards the *Duc* as he came towards her bed, looking, she thought, so magnificent in his evening clothes and at the same time so elegant that he might have come straight from a grand dinner party.

There was a smile on his lips, and she could see by the light of the candles that he looked happy and, she thought, younger.

"You are still awake?" he asked. "I hoped you would sleep."

He reached her side and stood looking down at her, and impulsively because she could not prevent herself she held out both her arms.

"You are . . safe! He . . did not . . hurt you?"

The *Duc* smiled and sat down on the bed taking her hands in his.

He kissed them and turned them over to kiss first one palm, and then the other.

It was something that had never happened to Arletta before and she felt a thrill seep through her that was like a streak of lightning.

As the *Duc* felt not only her fingers but her whole body quiver, he said:

"My precious, I have so many things to tell you, far more important than what has just happened."

"I . . I have to . . know."

He gave a sigh, then holding both her hands in his, he said:

"I took Byien and my Major Domo with me down to the dungeons where you and I left Jacques."

"He is . . alive?"

"Very much alive," the *Duc* answered, "and swearing

and cursing in a manner which has made me realise, as I should have done before, that his brain is unhinged."

"I thought he . . must be . . mad!"

"That is the kindest thing we can say about him."

"What have you . . done with . . him?"

"I have taken him to the Doctor who looks after everybody in the Castle. He has a small Hospital, a very small one, where the bullet which lodged in his shoulder when you shot him will be extractēd. However, I have made sure he will not escape from there, and tomorrow I will deal with his future."

"There will . . not be a . . trial?"

Arletta's voice trembled.

"Because I cannot have you involved in this, and also because, as you will understand, I wish to have no scandal surrounding my family, Jacques will be treated far better than he deserves."

"W.what do you . . mean?"

"I am planning to have him sent to an estate I own in French Colonial Africa. There he will stay working on a farm until he dies. If he returns to France he will be arrested."

The *Duc*'s voice was firm, but not hard, and Arletta said:

"I think you . . are being . . kind."

"As I have already said, far kinder than he deserves," the *Duc* agreed, "and very much kinder than the way he treated us."

"You had no notion that he was . . obsessed with the . . idea of taking . . your place?"

"I did not realise Jacques had killed my wife," the *Duc* said, "although I knew it was he who spread the rumour that I killed her because we quarrelled."

He paused and because she hated to think how much he had suffered from the whispering campaign against him, Arletta's fingers tightened on his.

"I guessed however that was what had happened," the

Duc continued, "when my friend Madeleine Montsarrat died of an overdose of Laudanum."

He paused and in a very small voice Arletta asked:

"Were you . . very much in love with . . her?"

"I loved her as much as I was capable of loving at that moment," the *Duc* admitted, "and I thought she would make me a very suitable wife and give me the children I wanted."

Again it seemed to Arletta that a knife pierced her heart.

She did not speak and the *Duc* went on:

"Then when I was aware that it was Jacques who was making me hated and feared, not only by everybody in the Castle, and on my estate, but in the world outside, I could not think of a way to stop him."

"Did you . . speak to him . . about it?" Arletta asked.

"What would have been the point?" he asked. "He would only have denied being the originator of such tales. I suppose too I was proud, too proud to argue and plead with a man I utterly despised."

"I can understand . . that."

She thought that it was the *Duc*'s pride that had made his tongue so sarcastic and his look so cynical, because he would not admit that he was being manipulated by his disreputable Cousin.

"Then you came," the *Duc* said in a low voice, "and I was really frightened."

"Frightened?"

It was a word Arletta would never have imagined him using.

He smiled before he said very gently:

"I fell in love with you, my alluring, fascinating little teacher, when I saw you dancing under the chandeliers in the Ball-Room, and wearing very little to hide your exquisite figure."

Arletta blushed, but was too shy to look at the *Duc* as she asked:

"Were you . . very shocked?"

"I was intrigued. At the same time I knew indisputably that I had found what I had been seeking all my life."

"How could you have . . known that?"

"You are not the only person, my lovely one, who is perceptive."

"I . . I knew you were that . . but not about . . me."

"I am very, very perceptive about you," the *Duc* said firmly. "At the same time, I realised that Jacques was watching us, and although I could hardly believe he would destroy you as he had already destroyed two other women in my life, I was desperately afraid."

He gave a deep sigh before he went on:

"I blame myself for not, as I ought to have done, sending you back to England as being a very unsuitable Governess."

Arletta gave a little cry.

"I was so afraid you . . might do that after you had . . seen me in the Ball-Room. But I wanted to . . stay here. I desperately wanted to . . stay."

"So you stayed," the *Duc* said, "But it might, if you had not saved us both, have been a tragedy for which nobody would ever have known the true explanation."

The way he spoke made Arletta say:

"We are safe, but promise me you will see that we remain so and he cannot . . escape to . . somehow try . . again."

"I swear to you that will never happen," the *Duc* answered, "and now my darling, I am free to ask you if you will be my wife."

Arletta stared at him. Then she said:

"Did you say . . are you really asking me to . . marry you?"

"I love you as I have never loved anybody before," the *Duc* said, "and I think you love me."

"It . . cannot be . . true!"

"It is true!" he insisted. "And as I do not intend to risk

143

losing you as I might have done tonight, I am determined to marry you immediately. Then I will be able to look after you a great deal better than I have done up until now."

There was a dazzling light in Arletta's eyes.

At the same time, because it was impossible for her to comprehend entirely what the *Duc* was saying to her she faltered:

"You cannot . . it is not right for you . . and you do not even . . know who . . I am."

The *Duc* laughed and it was a very happy sound.

"I know you are somebody I love, and who is everything I want in a woman, and who, although you may not realise it, is already part of my heart and my soul, if I have one!"

"B.but . . I am not . . J.Jane . . Turner!"

"I am well aware of that!"

"You are? But . . how?"

"Because, my beautiful one, Lady Langley, when she persuaded me to engage a Governess for David said;

" 'If you are worried that Miss Turner will disrupt your household in any way, let me assure you she is a very sensible young woman of twenty-eight, and rather plain, poor thing, so I am afraid no man will ever look at her, but she is very competent and kind.' "

The *Duc* smiled again as he said:

"Only the last two adjectives apply to you."

"So you . . guessed from the . . beginning that I was not . . Jane!"

"To begin with, by no stretch of the imagination could you be twenty-eight," the *Duc* said. "How old are you?"

"I am twenty."

"And your name?"

"Is Arletta. That is true. It slipped out by mistake."

"I guessed that too," he said, "and although it makes no difference to me who you are, I shall have to know the rest of your name before I fill in the forms that are compulsory in a French marriage."

"My name is Cherrington-Weir," Arletta said shyly.

144

"My father, who died only a few weeks ago, was the Sixth Earl of Weir."

She did not wait for the *Duc* to comment, but went on:

"What I have longed to tell you, because I felt you would be interested, was that my mother's mother was the *Comtesse* de Falaise who came from Normandy, and I was called after her."

She looked at the *Duc* apprehensively as she spoke, in case she had said anything wrong.

Then he exclaimed:

"I cannot believe it! The Falaises are directly related to my family, and we are therefore, my darling, of the same blood as well as being united in every other way."

Arletta gave a cry of delight.

"I am glad, so very, very glad! I think *Grandmère*, whom I adored, would be pleased too."

"So will my grandmother."

"I am sure if I really had been Jane Turner," Arletta replied, "she would have been shocked at her grandson making a marriage that could only be described as a *mèsalliance*. She made it quite plain that she suspected I had come here to 'catch' you!"

"That is exactly what you have done!" the *Duc* said. "Actually, *Grandmère* will be so grateful that you have saved my life that I think anything else about you would have paled into insignificance. But now she will, my precious, not that it matters, approve of you whole-heartedly."

"Can I . . really . . marry you?"

"I have every intention that you shall do so," the *Duc* said, "and although I have a great deal to teach you, my adorable little twenty-year-old, you have a lot to teach me."

She looked surprised and he explained:

"I have already had a few lectures from you, and now it is up to you to fill the Castle with love, and make certain it is as beautiful inside as it is out."

Arletta gave a deep sigh before she said:

"Can you . . really mean to marry me when you . . hate the English so ferociously?"

She was too shy to look at him as she asked the question, and she was suddenly afraid as he took his hand away from hers.

Then he said.

"I expected you to ask me that question and there is a lot of explaining to do as to why I hated your countrymen until you came and changed everything. Will you however, answer a question I am going to put to you?"

"Yes, of course," Arletta replied.

"Will you tell me," the *Duc* asked, "that you are aware, as I am, that nothing really matters except the love we know exists between us and which is different from anything else?"

Arletta was about to speak, but he went on:

"Nationality, family, social importance, titles, money, can any of them compare with what you felt just now when I kissed you, and what for me was an emotional experience I have never had before in the whole of my life?"

"Is that . . true?"

"I think you know what I am saying is the truth," the *Duc* said solemnly. "I adore you, Arletta, and I worship you because you are everything a woman should be, and whom I thought I would never find."

He spoke so solemnly, while every word vibrated in her heart, and Arletta put up her arms and pulled his head down to hers.

She had the feeling as she did so that he had deliberately not kissed her when he came into her Bedroom because he had thought it might make her shy or perhaps shocked.

Now she pulled him close to her and his lips were on hers.

Once again there was the rapture, the wonder, and the

146

ecstasy. As he carried her into the sky they were part of God.

Then when she wanted him to kiss her and go on kissing her, he deliberately moved and said:

"You are not to tempt me, *ma Belle*, until we are married. Then I can teach you about love without being afraid of frightening you or making you feel you are doing something that your mother and your grandmother would think was wrong."

The way he spoke made her remember the *Comte* and Arletta said:

"You are . . looking after . . me and . . protecting me."

"That is excatly what I intend to do," the *Duc* said. "And now I am going to tell you why I hated the English. But before I do so, there is one thing I want to say."

"What is . . it?" Arletta asked a little nervously.

They were talking, as they always had, in French, and now the *Duc* said quietly:

"*Je t'aime*! I cannot say it too often, and I will also say it in your language – I love you!"

He spoke in English and Arletta stared at him in amazement.

"You speak English?"

"Almost as well as you speak French."

"Is that . . true? I cannot . . believe it!"

"Then let me explain," he said. "The reason why I loathed the English was that my mother died when I was ten, and two years later my father married an Englishwoman."

Arletta gave a little gasp.

"An Englishwoman!"

"I should have said rather that *she* married *him*!" the *Duc* went on in a hard voice. "He was a sick man, broken in body and spirit because he had lost the wife he loved, and she tricked him into becoming his wife."

"I am . . sorry," Arletta said, knowing how much it had hurt him.

"She wanted," the *Duc* went on, "not only to be the *Duchesse* de Sauterre, but also to produce the next *Duc*, cutting me out. Because she was unable to do so owing to my father's bad health, she made my life a living hell. She tortured me as only a small, rather over-sensitive boy can be tortured, with a mental cruelty which made me loathe her. In fact, she was loathed by everybody in the Castle, including my grandmother."

"Why did nobody tell me this?" Arletta asked.

"When I was eighteen, just before my father died and I inherited the title, my Stepmother had a fatal riding accident!" the *Duc* replied. "Because her death was a relief and a deliverance, it was agreed that her name would never be mentioned again by those who had known her and her diabolical treatment of me."

"I am sorry . . so desperately sorry."

"You can therefore understand," the *Duc* went on, "that when my sister married an Englishman I opposed it with every means in my power, thinking that we all might have to suffer again from the cruelty and spite of somebody English."

His lips twisted in a faint smile as he said:

"Actually, Gerald was a very quiet, unassuming character, but my Stepmother's treatment of me had gone too deep for me to forget or forgive."

"Now I can . . understand," Arletta murmured.

"I knew you would," the *Duc* said, "and I confess I was wrong – completely and absolutely wrong – to try to turn David against his own countrymen and prevent him from going to his father's School."

Because he was naturally so proud, Arletta knew the admission was a tremendous effort, and she said very gently:

"You have made amends for all that. Can I really help you to . . forget what you have . . suffered?"

She looked at him anxiously as she went on:

"Suppose there is always some . . dark spot in our . .

love that I cannot . . change and which . . as the years go by . . make you . . hate me?"

The *Duc* laughed.

"Do you really think, my darling, that I could possibly hate you?" he asked in English. "I have already told you that I adore and worship you, and I know that you will bring me everything that is best in England, just as I will try to give you everything that is best in France."

"That is what I . . want to . . think," Arletta said, "and I will do . . everything I can do to make you . . happy."

"All you have to do is to love me," the *Duc* said solemnly. "But it is what I have missed since my mother died, and what I need desperately for myself, and one day for my children."

"I will give it to you . . I swear I will give it to you," Arletta cried.

Once again she held out her arms and the *Duc* kissed her.

She thought as he did so there was something holy and reverent in his kiss that had not been there before.

Then when he raised his head there was no longer any need for the light from the candles, for the first rays of the sun were coming through the East window illuminating the whole room with a golden light.

"Now I am going to leave you," he said, "and you are to go to sleep. Dream of me and forget all the horrors that have happened because they are not important."

"You will still be there in . . the morning?" Arletta asked. "You will not vanish and I will find this has . . all been a . . wonderful dream?"

"I will be there," the *Duc* said, "not only tomorrow, and the day after, but for the rest of our lives together."

He kissed her hand, then he rose, blew out the candles and walked towards the door.

"Goodnight, my perfect and most beloved wife-to-be," he said in English. "I love you!"

Then he was gone and Arletta felt tears of happiness running down her cheeks.

*　　*　　*

The little Church outside the great gates of the Castle was decorated with white lilies.

Apart from the bride and bridegroom and *Monsieur* Byien, who was the *Duc*'s Best Man, there was nobody else in the Church.

The village priest officiated with two servers, and Arletta felt that the empty aisles were filled with the spirits of those who had lived in the Castle for so many generations and worshipped there.

They had left behind them their prayers and faith of which she had been so vividly conscious the first time she had prayed in the old Church.

She had asked the *Duc* to see that all the candles were lit before the statue of Joan of Arc, and when he looked surprised she had said:

"I lit one the first time I came here, and I prayed that somehow the shadows over the Castle would go away, and I think too that in my heart I prayed for you."

"Then we must certainly be grateful," the *Duc* smiled.

Because he was of such importance the Mayor had come from the nearest town to the Castle earlier in the morning and had married them according to French Law.

After he left, the *Duc* had walked with Arletta across the great courtyard and into the Church.

He had announced that because Arletta was in mourning there would be no guests at the wedding.

But he had added that the staff from the Castle and everybody in the village would be entertained later in one of the huge rooms that were used for such occasions.

And as the Church was so small the bride and bridegroom would be married quietly and alone.

It was a slightly surprising arrangement, but the villagers would not think of disobeying the *Duc* and were appeased at being excluded from the ceremony by the fact that David and Pauline waited just outside the door to shower them with rose petals.

As soon as they realised what the children were about to do, the villagers picked the petals from every flower in their gardens.

When Arletta and the *Duc* came out through the great arched door they were enveloped so that their walk from the Church back to the Castle was literally, Arletta said with a smile, 'a path of roses'.

"That is what our life together will be," the *Duc* said.

The way he spoke and the love in his eyes made her feel as if she moved in the Fairyland which she had felt ever since she awoke.

The morning after the drama in the dungeon she had slept as she had not expected to until luncheon time.

It was the Housekeeper who had brought her a meal on a tray at one o'clock, saying:

"*Monsieur le Duc*'s orders, *M'mselle*, and you're to stay in bed until you're really rested."

"But . . it is so late!" Arletta protested. "I had no idea I could sleep so long!"

"It's certainly not surprising, *M'mselle*," the Housekeeper said in a repressed tone, "seeing all you've been through. But you must be sensible and realise it's a real shock to the system."

Arletta knew then that the whole household would be aware of what had happened.

It was one of the reasons why the *Duc* wished her to stay quietly in her room so as not to be involved in the explanations that would have to be made or in answering innumerable questions if she went downstairs.

She did in fact do what he wished, and only when he suggested that when she was dressed he would like to see her at five o'clock did she eagerly go down to his Study where he was waiting for her.

As she entered the room she stood for a moment just inside the door.

151

Then as he held out his arms she ran towards him, feeling there was no need for her to hear what had happened.

They were one, and she loved him so overwhelmingly that nothing else mattered.

They sat and talked for a long time. Then he said:

"I am going to send you back to bed, my darling. You have been through an experience which would leave most women prostrate, and I also have so many things to arrange that it is impossible to do them if you are beside me!"

"You do not want me?" Arletta asked provocatively.

"I will answer that question tomorrow, after we are married," he replied.

"Tomorrow?"

"I told you I was not going to wait any longer! You are mine, Arletta, and only when you are my wife will I feel no longer afraid of losing you."

She realised as he spoke that just as she had been horrified by the terror the *Comte* had inflicted on them in the dungeon, so for the *Duc*, because he loved her, it had been a ghastly experience to think he could not protect her as he wished to do.

She remembered how he had begged the *Comte* to spare her life, and she thought no man could be more wonderful or more loving.

She was prepared to allow him to know what was best for them both without argument.

In fact, she thought with a little smile, as she went back up to bed as he had virtually commanded, he would always be her master.

It would be impossible to fight against him, even though she might coax him with love into doing what she wanted.

She therefore went to bed, her whole being vibrating from the wonder of his kisses, and feeling that her head was in the clouds because of the plans he was making for them both.

"We will be married tomorrow," the Duke had said, "and on the following day we will leave for my Villa in the South of France where we shall be alone with nobody to disturb us, and I will tell you of my love."

"You . . know that is . . what I want," Arletta said with a little quiver of excitement in her voice. "At the same time . . we must not forget David!"

The *Duc* smiled.

"I thought that was something you would say, and I have not forgotten David. I have already arranged for an Englishman who is studying French at the University of Limoges to come here in our absence, and stay until we return, or perhaps longer, if you approve him."

As Arletta gave a cry of delight, the *Duc* added:

"Incidentally, he is very keen on cricket, and I suggested to him that he forms a team from amongst the footman and the other young men on the estate."

Arletta clasped her hands together.

"How can you be so . . wonderful as to think of . . everything?"

"I think of you," the *Duc* replied, and she knew that was the truth.

When she awoke very early on her wedding morning, she found he had thought of her in more ways than one.

The Housekeeper brought to the room a wedding gown which had been worn by the *Duc*'s mother on her wedding day, and which was only a trifle too large for her in the waist.

Otherwise it fitted her very well.

Of white satin with a very full skirt, the top was a lace bertha off the shoulders which was embroidered all over with tiny diamanté and pearls.

It was so lovely that Arletta could hardly believe when she saw herself in the mirror that it had not been specially designed for her.

With the exquisite Brussels lace veil which the de Sauterres had worn for generations and a diamond tiara, she looked like the Fairy Princess she had visualised herself as being when she had first come to the Castle.

When she came down from the tower for the last time, since tonight she would be in the State bedroom where the *Duchesses* de Sauterre had slept through the ages, there was a bouquet of white orchids for her to carry.

The *Duc* was waiting for her, dressed as was the custom for Frenchmen in full evening dress.

He looked so magnificent with a ribbon across his white shirt and a number of jewelled Orders on his coat, that Arletta could only gasp in admiration.

Then as he kissed her hand he said:

"You look as I wanted you to look – as my bride, and as the Saint who lives in a shrine in my heart."

After their wedding they went up to see the *Duchesse* and, as if she wanted to celebrate the occasion, she was festooned in even more jewellery than Arletta had ever seen her wear before.

She kissed the old lady and so did the *Duc*, and she said:

"You see? I was right! I knew you had come here to ensnare my grandson!"

"As I am very willing to be," the *Duc* smiled.

The *Duchesse* chuckled, then she said to Arletta:

"I have not only to thank you, my dear, for saving my grandson's life, but also for saving me from having to see his despicable Cousin take his place as the new *Duc*!"

"You are not to speak of it!" The *Duc* interposed.

"I have not yet finished, Etienne," the *Duchesse* said firmly. "I only wanted to tell Arletta that she is the best and most beautiful thing that has ever come to the Castle, and that we all love her, every one of us!"

Because she was so moved Arletta felt the tears come into her eyes.

Then when the *Duchesse* had drunk their health in champagne and they had kissed her again, they left the room.

The old maid was waiting outside.

"You've made *Madame* very happy, *Monsieur*," she said to the *Duc*. "I've never known her so thrilled or so delighted as she is today."

"That is what I am feeling myself," the *Duc* admitted, and he and Arletta went downstairs.

There was one more party to attend which was the luncheon arranged for the staff, tenants, and the labourers on the estate.

The huge room which, Arletta learnt, had once been where revels had taken place in Mediaeval times, was decorated with flowers and bunting.

There were long trestle tables, groaning with food, although how it had been organised so quickly she could not imagine until she learned that the Chefs had been working literally all night.

There was home-brewed cider as well as wine for everybody who wanted it, and David was particularly excited because the *Duc* had told him that in his absence he was to play host.

He sat at the top of one of the long trestle tables and Pauline at the other, and Arletta knew it was impossible for the two children to be more thrilled by the responsibilities which the *Duc* had given them.

The *Duc* made a speech thanking everybody for their congratulations and good wishes, and saying that a new era of happiness had begun at the castle and it was up to them to make sure everybody forgot the unhappiness of the last years.

As he spoke Arletta swore in her heart that she would make up for all everyone else had suffered.

They left the party to go back alone to their own luncheon which was arranged in one of the small rooms that Arletta had not seen before.

What she ate and drank she had no idea, because although while the servants were in the room they talked of ordinary things, the *Duc*'s eyes were telling her of his love.

It was impossible to think of anything but the sensations he aroused in her.

When at last they were alone she thought he would take her into the Study.

Instead they walked up the Grand Staircase towards the State-Rooms and now she thought he would perhaps take her to the Ball-Room where he had watched her dancing alone and said that it was there he fell in love.

However, he went on down the long corridor to where at the end was his own Bedroom, the most important in the whole house.

Next to it was the room which the Housekeeper had told Arletta she would occupy when she left the tower Bedroom.

David had not shown her these rooms on her tour of the house because the shutters were closed in the *Duchesse*'s room, and he was too nervous to take her into his Uncle's.

Now Arletta found the rooms were more beautiful than anything she could imagine in her dreams.

What was more, her room was decorated with white flowers which in contrast to the pale blue brocade walls made a perfect background for the colourful Fragonard pictures which were appropiately of lovers and cupids.

There was a huge canopied bed carved with cupids under a ceiling depicting Venus rising from the foam.

"I shall not feel . . real in such a beautiful room!" Arletta said in an awe-stricken little voice.

"Come and look at mine," the *Duc* said.

He opened a communicating door and she found that his room was even larger than hers.

It was decorated in almost the same manner, but was more masculine.

The bed was hung with curtains of red velvet with the de Sauterre crest over a carved and gilt headboard.

What was surprising, she thought, was that the flowers that decorated his room as well as hers were white orchids and lilies.

As she looked round she realised the *Duc* had shut the door and was now closer to her, and she thought he was about to kiss her.

Instead he lifted the tiara from her head and put it on top of a chest.

Then he took off her lace veil and threw it over a chair.

She waited, accepting that he wanted to do things his own way, but longing for him to kiss her. She felt as if her whole body was pulsating with a strange rapture while she waited for him to do so.

Instead he drew the hairpins from her hair and it fell over her shoulders in soft waves.

"Now you look as you did the first time I saw you," he said in a deep voice, "except, my darling, that you have on far more clothes than you had then!"

"Y.you are . . making me feel . . shy," Arletta said in a hesitating little voice.

"I adore you when you are shy."

As if he could wait no longer, he lifted her chin and his lips were on hers.

As he kissed her and the rapture within her heart began to leap up to her lips, she felt him undoing her gown.

A moment later it fell like a soft sigh to the ground.

He picked her up in his arms and carried her to the big bed.

For a moment she did not really understand what was happening; she only felt a wild excitement sweep over her that seemed to be part of the beat of her heart.

And yet her love was more than that.

It was in her mind and in her soul and they all belonged to the *Duc*.

He laid her down against the lace-trimmed pillows and drew the sheet over her.

Then, as the sunshine coming in through the windows which overlooked the gardens and the fountains seemed to blind her eyes, he was beside her.

His arms were around her and she felt herself trembling with the wonder of it.

She knew that he, too, was feeling as if the angels were singing and already they had left the earth and were flying into the sky.

"*Je t'aime*! I love you!" the *Duc* said.

His lips were on hers and his hand was touching her body and she could feel his heart beating against hers.

"Teach . . me . . Oh, teach me about . . love," she whispered.

Then she knew there was no language on earth in which they could express what they felt for each other.

But there was no need for words.

Their love was life itself, the life which came from God and which was to be theirs for Eternity.

Barbara Cartland
Love Comes West £1.25

Roberta thought her adventures were over when she left Algiers to begin a new life in California. Yet there she met a sadistic preacher, a penniless painter, and an eccentric millionaire – not forgetting an orphan boy and a hungry puppy. Her head often ruled her heart, but not when it came to posing for Adam and running away. When Adam's burning kisses sealed their reunion Roberta knew the light of love would shine from his every canvas.

Revenge of the Heart £1.25

Considering he had saved her from drowning, Nadia felt she had no option but to comply with Warren's request that she pose as his fiancée and accompany him to England. At Buckwood House new dangers threaten Nadia as she falls more and more in love with the Marquis. And only much later can she reveal the secrets of her past and seek new happiness in Warren's gentle kisses.

A Very Unusual Wife £1.50

The reputation of the Marquis of Falcon was such that Queen Victoria would bestow no further honour on him until he was married. His offer for the youngest daughter of the Earl of Warnborough brought him many surprises, not least Elmina's use of karate to repel his unwanted advances on their wedding night. Only when Elmina's life is in danger does the Marquis realise his love for her, and ride like a whirlwind to answer her silent prayers.

Barbara Cartland
Tempted to Love £1.25

With her heart pounding, Ivona hurried into the bedroom. Taking off her nun's habit she began to struggle into the young man's trousers . . . After the death of her mother, the Lady Ivona is condemned by her uncle and guardian to become a postulant in a severe convent. Travelling across Alsace, she manages to elude her escort, and shares an unexpected refuge with the Duc de Sancerre . . .

Fire in the Blood £1.25

Following the death of her father, Pandia is amazed to receive a surprise visit from her twin sister. Selene wishes Pandia to impersonate her at a country funeral while she keeps an illicit assignation. Unhappily and apprehensively, Pandia agrees. At church she meets Lord Silvester Stone and each is attracted to the other. As Pandia hurries back to London to find Selene's husband unexpectedly returned, Silvester is prepared to sacrifice the whole world for Pandia's love.